'You're ea[rly]' [she said] accusingly.

James's eyes twinkled as his smile broadened. 'Like you, I'm an early bird.'

'Out to catch the unsuspecting worm?' Her voice came out sharp, scathing.

Immediately the smile disappeared. 'Accusing me of spying on your precious staff, Sister?' he asked in a silky voice. 'Because I can assure you that nothing was further from my mind. I like everything up-front when dealing with my colleagues.

Margaret O'Neill started scribbling at four and began nursing at twenty. She contracted TB and, when recovered, did her British Tuberculosis Association nursing training before general training at the Royal Portsmouth Hospital. She married, had two children, and with her late husband she owned and managed several nursing homes. Now retired and living in Sussex, she still has many nursing contacts. Her husband would have been delighted to see her books in print.

Recent titles by the same author:

A CAUTIOUS LOVING
MORE THAN SKIN-DEEP
THE GENEROUS HEART
DOWNLAND CLINIC

DOUBLE TROUBLE

BY
MARGARET O'NEILL

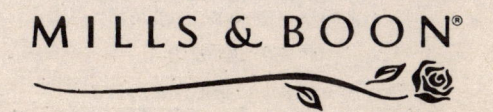

MILLS & BOON

DID YOU PURCHASE THIS BOOK WITHOUT A COVER?
If you did, you should be aware it is **stolen property** as it was reported *unsold and destroyed* by a retailer. Neither the Author nor the publisher has received any payment for this book.

All the characters in this book have no existence outside the imagination of the author, and have no relation whatsoever to anyone bearing the same name or names. They are not even distantly inspired by any individual known or unknown to the author, and all the incidents are pure invention.

All Rights Reserved including the right of reproduction in whole or in part in any form. This edition is published by arrangement with Harlequin Enterprises II B.V. The text of this publication or any part thereof may not be reproduced or transmitted in any form or by any means, electronic or mechanical, including photocopying, recording, storage in an information retrieval system, or otherwise, without the written permission of the publisher.

This book is sold subject to the condition that it shall not, by way of trade or otherwise, be lent, resold, hired out or otherwise circulated without the prior consent of the publisher in any form of binding or cover other than that in which it is published and without a similar condition including this condition being imposed on the subsequent purchaser.

MILLS & BOON and MILLS & BOON with the Rose Device are registered trademarks of the publisher.

*First published in Great Britain 1997
Harlequin Mills & Boon Limited,
Eton House, 18-24 Paradise Road, Richmond, Surrey TW9 1SR*

© Margaret O'Neill 1998

ISBN 0 263 80705 3

*Set in Times 10 on 11½ pt. by
Rowland Phototypesetting Limited
Bury St Edmunds, Suffolk*

03-9803-50007-D

*Printed and bound in Great Britain
by Mackays of Chatham PLC, Chatham*

CHAPTER ONE

THE phone rang as Kate, having completed her morning round, arrived back in her office.

She picked up the receiver.

'Sister,' the administrator's voice, flat and formal, came over briskly. 'Will you please come to my office?'

'What now? Oh, Grace, can't it wait? I've oodles to do.'

The reply came back sharply, 'So, what's new? And, no, it can't wait. Dr Bruce's here and he wants to meet you.' The administrator paused, and added silkily, mendaciously, 'And I know how much you've been looking forward to meeting our new medical director, Kate.'

Like hell I have, thought Kate, wryly, and well you know it, Grace Lyons. And you've not been looking forward to his arrival any more than I have so stop putting on a line for his benefit.

She took a deep breath. 'All right, Miss Lyons, I'll be with you in a few minutes. I've just got to sort a few things out with Staff on the med wing before I come up. I'm covering for Josie Styles today.' She made her voice as stiff and formal as Grace's had been.

'Right, expect you soon.'

Meg Short, the senior staff nurse on the medical wing, was giving out medicines from the secure trolley. Kate pulled a humorous face and raised her eyes heavenwards when she reached her.

'I've been summoned upstairs by the powers that be,' she explained, 'so we'll have to put off the teaching round till later. You get cracking on the dressings and take one of the assistants with you. I *hope* I won't be too long.'

Meg grinned. 'That was said from the heart. Expecting trouble, Sister?'

Kate hesitated. What was she expecting? 'Not exactly,' she said cautiously. There was not much she could or would say to a junior colleague, however trusted. 'I'm just wary. I'm about to meet our new medical director.'

Meg opened her eyes wide. 'The dashing Dr Bruce, quite a hunk if you like them tall, broad and chunky—and who doesn't? I thought he wasn't due to start till next week.'

'He's not, as far as I know,' said Kate. 'He's just turned up out of the blue, and I've been bidden to meet the great man.'

'Of course you missed him last week when he did a royal walkabout with the trustees and some local GPs in tow. You were off with this freak tummy bug, otherwise you would have been on the welcoming committee.'

Kate groaned. 'Don't remind me. The first time I've been off sick for yonks and it had to be that day. *If* he noticed my absence he probably thinks I was skiving.'

'What—you skive? My God, you're a workaholic *and* a slave-driver.' She chuckled and looked affectionately at her superior, for whom she had a lot of respect. 'I don't know how you do it—all this.' She waved her hand round the unit with its four-bedded cubicles. 'And the rest of the hospital and a home and kids to look after.'

'Plenty of women work and run homes—they have to.' Kate shrugged.

'Well, it's not for me. I'm not going to sacrifice myself to some undeserving guy,' Meg retorted fiercely. 'At least, not unless he's incredibly rich and can support me way above the manner to which I am accustomed.'

That's what we all say when we're young, thought Kate, believing that we can pick and choose who we fall in love with, and then someone comes along and blows common sense to smithereens.

'And quite right, too. Hold onto that dream,' she said with a laugh. 'Now, I'd better push off and get this meeting over. Wish me luck.'

'Fingers and toes crossed,' said Meg.

But she was puzzled. Why did Sister, one of the senior people at the hospital, need luck because she was going to see the administrator? It couldn't be that. True, admin and nursing staff didn't always see eye to eye, but Miss Lyons wasn't bad as administrators go and she and Kate Brown were good friends as well as senior colleagues. They practically ran the place between them.

So she must be nervous about meeting the new man, the dishy Dr Bruce. Incredible, she just wasn't the nervous sort. She took everything in her stride—she could handle anything. She'd soon have him tamed—or would she? From the fleeting glimpse she'd had of him last week he'd looked very together, very—commanding—distinguished? Boss-type material.

Could be that was what was bothering Sister Brown— that he'd want to take over and nice as she was, she wouldn't take that lying down.

Well, we'll find out soon enough if he's going to throw his weight about, she reminded herself philosophically, so get on with your work, Meg Short, and forget the power struggle at the top.

Ignoring the lift, to put off the dread moment of the meeting, Kate made her way up to Admin on the third— top—floor of the hospital. She reflected, not for the first time, as she climbed the wide easy stairs how pleasant it was to work in a building that was human size.

The Millchester Memorial Cottage Hospital, our hospital, she thought protectively. Built by the people of Millchester, it had room to spread outwards not upwards—and no newly appointed medical director is going to spoil that and turn it into a faceless, soulless monster of a high-rise, high-tech building.

She paused at the picture window on the third floor and looked out over the garden. Green lawns and flower-beds, blazing with colour, bordered the wide drive which swept up from the busy coast road. The road separated the hospital from the crescent-shaped bay beyond. She could see the sea, glittering in the spring sunshine, between the trees and above them—stretching away to the distant horizon.

The gatehouse at the foot of the drive was visible too, a trim, neat gabled building, relic of the old cottage hospital. She smiled with pleasure at the sight of it. Home, she mused, my home and my children's home—warm, comfortable, safe, and please, God, let it remain so. Don't let this newcomer spoil things.

Reluctantly she turned away from the window, marched along the corridor and knocked on the administrator's door.

Grace's voice called to her to come in.

Kate opened the door and stood just inside for a moment, registering the scene.

Grace was seated as usual at her desk. Her cleverly blended silver-grey ash-blonde hair, coiled into a neat chignon, gleamed healthily in the morning sunshine that flooded the room. Her angular but attractive face was turned in an intense listening mode towards the man sitting at the other side of the desk.

She didn't look fifty-something and she didn't look in the least bit hostile towards the man sitting opposite, the man whose appointment they'd both dreaded. Rather, she seemed fascinated by what he was saying.

He's won her round, thought Kate. He must have softened her up when they met last week and has completed the job today. Oh, Grace, some friend you are. How could you? You don't want the man here any more than I do. OK, so we've got to extend the usual courtesies, but do you have to hang on his every word?

He stood up as Kate entered, and smiled. It was an illuminating smile, wide and friendly, a smile that lit up a craggy, strongly masculine face with a rather prominent nose and deep-set hazel-green eyes beneath thick dark brows. He was as Meg had described—tall, broad and chunky with rich, dark, mahogany-brown hair springing from a high wide forehead, well cut but a little on the long side and beginning to curl against his collar.

Grace beckoned her forward. 'Come in, Kate, come and meet Dr Bruce, our new medical director.' She flashed both Kate and the doctor a smile.

'James,' he said, his smile widening even further. 'We missed each other last week. You were off sick.' His voice was deep and grainy, with a slight Scottish burr. He extended a deeply tanned hand.

Kate slipped hers, small and pale by comparison, into his and allowed her lips to curve slightly. 'Kate Brown,' she said coolly. 'Welcome to Millchester, Dr Bruce.' It was a hollow welcome. For the life of her she couldn't breathe any warmth into her voice. Did he sense that?

'James,' he repeated. He bent his head and peered at her name-tag pinned to the front of her uniform dress, and lightly tapped it with his forefinger. 'And it doesn't say "Kate" here.' His eyes gleamed. 'It says, "Sister Katrina Brown, Senior Nursing Supervisor". Katrina's such a pretty name—it suits you admirably. What a great pity you don't use it.'

His eyes flickered over her bob of burnished chestnut hair, high cheek-bones, determined chin and heavily fringed violet-blue eyes.

The inference he was making, thought Kate, was obvious—pretty name, pretty woman. Well, that was true, she acknowledged without false modesty, for, though no raving beauty, she knew she was reasonably pretty, had good bone structure, a healthy complexion and looked in her twenties rather than her thirties.

But the nerve of the man, ladling on the charm when they'd only just met. Did he expect her to respond in kind and tell him that he was a gorgeous hunk? And how would he react if she did? Who the hell did he think he was— God's gift to the nursing profession? She'd met his sort before.

Well, he might have bowled Grace over, but he wasn't going to do the same to her. It would take more than pretty speeches to do that. She would give him all the professional support that his position as director demanded, but no way did she have to *like* him or even pretend to like him.

She drew herself up to her full five feet five, her eyes flashed angrily and the nostrils of her neat retroussé nose quivered. 'Well, I don't use it. I'm known as Kate or Sister Brown to my colleagues. Take your pick, Dr Bruce.'

'Kate!' exclaimed Grace, clearly shocked by her angry tone. 'I'm sure James didn't mean—'

'To be rude and patronising,' interrupted the doctor. He stopped smiling. 'No, I didn't mean to be,' he said wryly. 'But I can quite see that it might have sounded that way.' He met Kate's flashing blue eyes. 'I apologise. It was impertinent of me to say what I did, though I meant it as a compliment. Am I forgiven?'

Did he mean it or was he speaking tongue-in-cheek? Kate looked hard into the hazel-green eyes flecked with gold. They were no longer amused, twinkling, but rather sombre. He sounded genuinely sorry that he'd offended her and she found herself rather regretting her knee-jerk reaction. Perhaps she was being over-sensitive, not because of the man but because of what he represented—a new boss, a new broom sweeping clean.

She let go of her anger, and said quietly, 'Of course. Let's forget it.'

'Thank you.' He nodded gravely. 'And, as you've forgiven me, could I persuade you to give me a tour of the hospital and put me in the picture about patient care and treatment? That is, if you can spare the time. Last week's walkabout was just window shopping, and what I want is to get the feel of things—and you're the person to help me do that.' He gave her a rueful smile. 'Or would I be pushing my luck?'

Don't smooth-talk me, thought Kate impatiently, but answered evenly. 'Not at all. I'd be pleased to show you around. I dare say the hospital won't grind to a halt if I rearrange my workload and catch up with the backlog later.' It wasn't the most gracious of replies but, then, he had put her on the spot and made it impossible for her to refuse him.

Grace looked furious, and said frostily. 'If there's a problem, Sister, I'll take Dr Bruce round the wards and introduce him to a few people, and you can fill him in on the nursing angle later.'

Hell, thought Kate, the wretched man really has won over our dedicated career woman. Who'd have thought Grace, of all people, would fall for his obvious charms? She's protecting him like a mother hen, and no longer sees him as a threat to the way we run the Memorial—but I do. He's not blinkered me.

But she mustn't upset Grace. After all, she was a friend

as well as a senior colleague. She tried to think of a suitable, placatory remark to make, but before she could frame the words the doctor interrupted.

'Look, forget it, ladies. I shouldn't even be here since I'm not due to start work till next week. It's not fair to upset your busy schedules. I'll push off now and see you on Monday in my office. I'll be there at eight.' He paused. 'And I'd be pleased, Sister. . .' he inclined his head slightly toward Kate '. . .if you'll spare me a couple of hours then to show me round and tell me all I need to know.'

It was a command rather than an invitation, the new boss pulling rank—making his presence felt. The smiling, accommodating, pleasant man had disappeared. This man was granite-faced and his voice was expressionless. It was impossible to tell if he was angry, disappointed or even, perhaps, hurt.

The last possibility shook Kate. She certainly hadn't intended to hurt the man. She'd just wanted to let him know that as nursing supervisor she was a busy woman with responsibilities. But of course he knew that and had acknowledged it. She hadn't needed to make a point of it, and she certainly shouldn't have been rude.

She owed him an apology.

She took a deep breath, tilted her head right back so that her eyes met his directly and said with quiet sincerity, 'I'm sorry. I must have sounded dreadfully rude. Please do stay. I'd like to show you around. The Memorial's a very special hospital and I love showing it off, especially to professionals who can appreciate what a super place it is—small, but well equipped and efficient.'

James stared down into the depths of her extraordinary violet-blue eyes. They were still fierce, but pleading with him to accept her offer to make amends. A surprising thought flitted through his mind—that she was like a lioness protecting her young or, in this case, her hospital. Well, he could appreciate that sort of loyalty.

No wonder she resented his arrival. She probably expected him to play the arrogant male in this largely female establishment, and sweep in and make dramatic changes, destroying what she and Grace Lyons had created and held together.

It would be up to him to convince her that he would do no such thing, and any changes would come about gradually and with her co-operation. Last week, and today from the administrator, he'd heard glowing reports about her efficiency and her popularity with staff and patients, and he had no wish to step on her or anyone else's toes. It was important that they should work together for the good of the hospital, and he damned well meant to do just that.

If only she hadn't been so bloody awkward over his request to look round her precious domain, and made it so clear how much she resented him. That had, surprisingly, hurt. He hadn't expected to be welcomed with open arms, but such open hostility was difficult to take. Still, she was trying hard to rescue the situation by making a very generous apology, and that couldn't have been easy. The least he could do was accept it with good grace.

He made his facial muscles relax, and allowed his lips to curve into a wide lopsided smile which was reflected in his eyes. 'Then I'd like to take you up on your offer, *Sister Kate Brown*,' he said, softly emphasising her name.

Kate felt herself blushing, something she hadn't done for a long time. 'Thank you,' she murmured.

'For what?'

'For accepting my apology and overlooking my initial reluctance to show you round. It was an unreasonable attitude to take.'

He shrugged, but kept his eyes fixed on hers. 'But not

surprising. Why should you put out the red carpet? You see me as an interloper in your precious hospital. I can appreciate that. You've been here since it opened. It's been your baby as far as overall patient care is concerned.'

Kate raised her eyebrows. He was being almost too understanding, too silver-tongued.

'I did have help from the local GPs, visiting consultants and a super nursing and support staff,' she said tartly.

'But you were ultimately responsible,' he persisted. 'Always here, always on the spot.'

'Yes,' she agreed.

'So, will you accept that I appreciate your position and want only to co-operate with you? Surely that's the basis for a good working partnership?'

Should she trust him? Did he mean what he said, or did he want to win her over for his own ends, whatever they might be? Not that she really had any option—they *had* to work together for the foreseeable future. She really did wish that she could be less suspicious, and take to him as Grace seemed to have done.

'Shall we shake on it?' he said, and again held out a large well-kept hand, and again, this time feeling slightly self-conscious, she put hers into it.

Startling them both, for in the heat of their exchange they had almost forgotten her presence, Grace Lyons gave a theatrical sigh of relief and said with dry humour, 'Well, thank goodness you've sorted things out between you. Now *go*, people, *go* before you change your minds, and please let me get on with my work.'

She was tremendously relieved that they had reached some sort of agreement. It would have been disastrous had Kate not squashed her antagonism. Antagonism that she understood and had shared, prior to meeting James Bruce. Like Kate, she had regarded his appointment with some dismay but now she felt reassured that it was not his intention to make dramatic changes to their beloved hospital and upset the smooth routine that they had established.

He would, she was sure, be an asset, not the liability that she and Kate had foreseen, and she was looking forward to working with him. And the hospital, though it would never be huge, thank God, was growing to meet the increasing demands of the town, and she and Kate needed a third dedicated person to share the responsibility of the day-to-day workload.

She picked up a pen, perched her fashionable half-rim glasses on her nose and peered over them at the doctor and Kate. 'You two still here?' she said.

James chuckled. 'OK, we can take a hint.' He placed his hand on Kate's back at waist level and steered her towards the door.

Kate stiffened, very conscious of the warmth of his palm and the pleasant sensation that radiated from it, a steady pulsing spreading up her spine and under her ribcage.

What the hell? She almost shrugged his hand away, but stopped herself.

He wasn't being familiar, she realised. It was just a casual, almost automatic movement on his part, a protective masculine gesture made without thinking, and she mustn't react to it as if it was something special or something to be resented. She forced herself to relax and let him guide her across the room.

He paused in the doorway and turned to thank Grace for having made him welcome.

'Think nothing of it—it was a pleasure. We look forward to having you here at the Memorial, James. Now tootle off and enjoy this fact-finding tour Kate's going to give you.'

'Oh, I'm sure I will,' he said dryly, his hand pressing

a little more firmly against Kate's back. 'Sister Brown—' his hazel eyes teased as he looked down at her '—will make sure that I'm fully clued in before I start work next week so I'll have no excuse for falling down on the job. I think we'll find that on all matters medical we're on the same wavelength.'

And with a gentle shove he propelled her in front of him through the open doorway into the corridor.

The corridor was empty but a murmur of voices, shrilling telephones and the general hum of office noises came from behind several closed doors.

To her chagrin, Kate missed the warm pressure of his hand when he dropped it from her back as they stood side by side outside Grace's office.

She said hurriedly, feeling breathless, 'Well, I suppose we'd better begin our tour up here. Obviously, as you must know, this is the admin floor. These are all offices...' she waved her hand down the length of the corridor lined with a dozen or so shut doors '...where the patients' files, X-rays and other documents are stored, and the accounts and so on are done.'

She pointed to the door next to Grace's. 'And Joy Nicholls, Grace's secretary, has this office next door to hers, and the senior accountant's office is next door to that. And the boardroom, where we have our weekly staff meeting with the trustees and where the VIPs are entertained, is at the end of the corridor.'

She shrugged. 'And that's about it,' she finished lamely. 'Sorry, but I don't know what else to tell you. They're just offices.'

James was looking down his rather beaky nose at her, his wide mouth quirking at the corners and his eyes gleaming with amusement.

He raised one eyebrow. 'Boring, isn't it?' he said.

'Admin. Necessary but boring. Not like our line of business, dealing with patients, satisfying hands-on medical stuff.'

Kate breathed in a huge sigh of relief, and expelled it slowly. She almost smiled. 'So you don't want to call in at each office and meet the admin staff?' she asked. Then she clapped a hand over her mouth. 'Oh, Lord, that sounds awful. They're such a nice crowd, but—'

'They're not doctors or nurses, dealing with your precious patients. And, no, I don't need to look around up here. Grace introduced me to everyone earlier.'

'Of course, it's her department and she loves it. She actually finds facts and figures and computer printouts about costings and so on exciting. Isn't it amazing?'

'Amazing,' agreed James, his eyes dancing with amusement. 'The only computer printouts that excite me are cardiographs and lab tests and such, directly related to a patient's condition, and the less I have to do with this side of modern medicine the better.'

For the first time since they'd met Kate saw him as a possible ally rather than the enemy, and gave him a tentative smile. Perhaps, she thought warily, as he had said, they were on the same wavelength medically speaking. Well, only time would tell. He had a long way to go before he proved himself to her.

'That's exactly how I feel,' she said. 'But thank goodness Grace loves the admin side of things. Someone's got to do it. She's a super person to work with. A buffer between the board and medical needs at grass-roots level. If I tell her that we need more nursing help on the surgical unit because we can't cope efficiently otherwise she does battle till we get another nurse or an assistant or whatever.'

'An unusual administrator, to say the least. I thought they were all into economy drives and cost-cutting.'

'Oh, Grace is tough when it comes to making sensible economies, but she knows that the priority should be on patient care and, to be fair, because this is both publicly and privately funded so do most of the board.'

'I gathered that. I wouldn't have considered working here otherwise.' James grasped her elbow firmly. 'Now,' he said, 'let's go down into *our* world and start meeting patients.'

A short corridor, opening off the main first-floor corridor, led to the surgical unit of twenty beds. This was divided, like the medical ward on the ground floor, into four-bedded bays grouped round the nurses' station in the centre. The ward faced south, overlooking Millchester Sands. The unit was light and airy with pretty divider curtains between each bed.

'We do elective surgery on Tuesdays and Thursdays,' explained Kate, as they stood just inside the swing doors by the office at the entry of the ward. 'And many patients receiving minor surgery, but not suitable for day surgery, are only in for a night. Wednesday is the major change-over day, with quite a few patients being discharged and those for the next day's list being admitted.'

'And today's Wednesday so Ward Sister's going to be up to her eyes in work. I don't want to be a nuisance,' James said, surprising her by his thoughtfulness. 'The last thing she'll want is us, wandering around and getting in the way. Look, I'm quite happy to wait till I'm in harness next week to get to know my way around here, though I would like you to introduce me to Sister, just briefly.'

'Oh, Dora Cross won't consider you a nuisance,' Kate replied, with a little laugh. 'She's of the old school and believes that, until proved otherwise, all doctors are worth their salt and should be extended every courtesy and treated with a great respect.'

'And do *you* think I'll be worth my salt, Sister Brown?' he asked, raising quizzical eyebrows. But he wasn't being funny, as his eyebrows suggested. His voice was deadly serious, and so were his eyes.

He really wants my opinion, thought Kate in astonishment.

She swallowed her surprise and said softly, 'That remains to be seen, Dr Bruce. It'll be up to you.' Was that going too far? After all, he was the medical director, not a young green houseman fresh out of medical school. It wasn't up to her to make judgements, even though he'd invited one.

'So I've got to prove myself, hmm?'

She breathed a sigh of relief. He didn't seem to have been offended by her remark. 'Something like that,' she said, half joking, half serious. 'But first you must pass the acid test and win Dora's initial approval. But, I warn you, her standards are sky high and she goes a bundle on instinct and first impressions.'

James pulled a comically despairing face, turning down his mouth at the corners, and raised his eyebrows again. This time he *was* being funny. 'She sounds a bit of a witch, a soothsayer, a formidable lady, and you think I'm not going to pass muster,' he said ruefully.

Kate dimpled. Well, there was no doubt that he had a nice sense of humour and didn't mind turning it on himself.

'I didn't say that,' she said. 'I think you're in with an even chance.'

But she guessed that he was in with a more than fifty-fifty chance, and the perceptive Sister Cross, tough as she was, would be won over.

It wasn't just his charm, his friendliness, that would win

her over—Dora would see through that in an instant. But it was what lay beneath that her famed instinct would suss out, and Kate was beginning to suspect that there might be more to Dr Bruce than just superficial charm. For, in spite of his smooth tongue—reluctant as she was to admit it—this man, whose arrival she had dreaded, did not appear to be the ruthless arrogant medic she'd expected but a caring doctor.

As she knocked at the ward office door she found herself hoping that this was what her older colleague, with her famous instinct, would confirm.

Which is exactly what happened. Within a few minutes of their meeting Kate could see that the doctor had got over the initial hurdle and won Dora's approval.

The small, brisk, dumpling of a woman, with close-cropped grey hair, surveyed him through snappy black eyes. 'I understand that you're a surgeon as well as a physician, Dr Bruce,' she said in her blunt fashion. 'Does that mean that you're going to operate here?'

'I hope so. Part of my brief is to relieve the local GPs who've been dealing with minor ops to date, and assist consultant surgeons who come in to operate on middle-range conditions. I believe that with the growth of the local community they are under some pressure.'

'We don't do any fancy surgery, you know—it's mostly hernias, vein-stripping, lumpectomies, haemorrhoidectomies and that sort of thing. Major ops, such as transplant surgery, go along the coast to Porthampton University Hospital, though we often do prior investigations and preparatory work here.'

'So I understand.'

'And you don't mind that? You don't hanker after making a spectacular breakthrough and making medical history?' She looked at him searchingly.

James smiled at her and fleetingly at Kate, catching her eyes, his own full of amusement. Is this a catch question? he seemed to be saying. He shook his head. 'Not at all,' he said. 'All surgery's important, whether it's a simple tonsillectomy or a multiple bypass. At the end of the day it's the patient who counts. And small local hospitals like this, which reduce the time that patients have to wait for treatment, are invaluable.'

It was an impeccable answer.

Sister Cross nodded. 'Quite right,' she said briskly, giving him one of her rare smiles. 'You'll do, Dr Bruce, you'll do. Now, if you'll excuse me, I must get on with the perennial paperwork. Kate will show you around. I look forward to working with you.' With a brisk handshake, she dismissed them from the office.

The doctor chuckled as they walked down the corridor and into the ward. 'Do you think I passed muster?' he asked.

'With flying colours,' said Kate dryly, leading him towards the nurses' station halfway down the ward.

She introduced him to Molly May, who was perched on a stool behind the desk. 'Staff Nurse May,' she explained. 'Sister's right-hand woman.'

'Nice to meet you, Staff,' said James with a smile. 'I'd like to look round, if I may, but I know you're busy so I'll try not to get in the way.'

Molly glowed and returned his smile. 'Oh, I'm sure you won't do that, Doctor,' she said, 'but I'm afraid I'll not be able to accompany you—I'm tied up here.'

'Not to worry, Staff, I'll be in safe hands. Sister Brown will be my guide and mentor.'

'And make a jolly good job of it, Doctor,' she said, grinning at Kate with an affectionate sort of lucky-old-you expression. 'Sister is very much a hands-on sort of supervisor and as on the ball about the ward as I am, aren't you Sister?'

'I like to keep myself clued in,' said Kate, colouring faintly at the unsolicited praise. 'And I sometimes fill in for Sister Cross when she's off,' she explained to the doctor, 'so Staff and I are used to working together.'

James slanted a smile as her as they moved away from the station. 'You obviously have a great rapport with your senior nurses,' he said softly. 'And it's clearly reflected in the rest of the staff—I noticed that when I was here last week. Everyone looks so happy. You must have worked damned hard to build up this sort of goodwill.'

'We work as a team,' Kate replied. 'We all started more or less together from the time the hospital opened. I picked the best of the profession, choosing with care both the registered and assistant nurses. They're a super crowd.'

'Led from the top,' said the doctor dryly. 'I do congratulate you, Kate.' He paused, and put a hand on her arm. 'And I hope that in time you will accept me as part of the team. Believe me, I have no intention of throwing my weight around. I just want to fit in.'

Kate looked down at his hand as it rested on her bare forearm, warm, reassuring, as his palm had felt on her back earlier, and then up into his gold-flecked green eyes. He looked back at her steadily. He sounded sincere, but did he mean it or was he simply saying what he knew she wanted to hear? Was it just his silver tongue talking?

She knew all about silver tongues. She thought about her ex-husband, and writhed inwardly. It was four years since they'd finally parted, but it still hurt to recall the years of deception, the skilful words cajoling, pleading, time after time, winning her trust.

Was James Bruce that sort of man? She continued to stare at the large, calm man standing beside her. He had convinced Grace of his good intentions, and Dora Cross approved of him. So why should she doubt him?

But I don't, she suddenly realised, I don't doubt him—at least, not as a doctor, and that's all that matters. I believe him when he says that he just wants to be part of the team.

She nodded, her eyes softening as she gave him her warmest smile yet. 'I'm sure you will. . .fit in, that is,' she said softly.

He grinned broadly, revealing strong even teeth that gleamed white against his dark tan. 'Thank you, that's the nicest thing you've said to me since we first met.' He dropped his hand from her arm. 'And now I suppose we'd better get cracking on the round. Lead on, Sister Brown.'

Kate introduced him to various patients as they made their way round the ward, giving him potted histories of the conditions and the surgery they had received or were to undergo the following day.

He chatted briefly to all of them and listened to what they had to say, answering questions and making reassuringly appropriate but honest and straightforward replies.

He paused at the end cubicle to speak to the old gentleman who was sitting beside his bed with his feet elevated on a stool. He had a round rosy face, thinning silvery hair and pale blue alert eyes. He was wearing hearing aids in both ears.

'This is Mr Carter,' murmured Kate to James. She bent over the elderly patient so that her face was on a level with his, and explained, 'This is Dr Bruce, Bob. He's the new medical director.'

She straightened up and said to James, 'Mr Carter's a strong supporter of our League of Friends, and has been helping to raise funds to rebuild the old cottage hospital for years. He's a retired gardener, but still does some voluntary part-time work here when he's up to it. As you see, he's deaf, but lip-reads if you speak clearly. He's having excision of bilateral hallux valgus tomorrow.'

James crouched down beside the old man, smiled and said, enunciating carefully, 'You've got problems with your feet, Mr Carter.'

'Bunions,' replied Mr Carter, in the flat tones of the very deaf. 'And they're giving me gyp.' He pushed off large, floppy slippers to expose pale feet with badly deformed, reddened big toe joints.

'Ouch, nasty. I see what you mean,' mouthed James slowly, running sensitive fingers over the inflamed joints. 'You'll be glad to get this operation done tomorrow. Not that you'll be out of the woods straight away. You're going to be pretty uncomfortable for a while, and learning to walk with splinted toes isn't going to be a picnic, old chap.' His lips framed the words clearly.

The faded blue eyes gleamed for an instant. 'Don't you worry about me, Doctor. I'll cope with that. I came through the war, army boots and all—Dunkirk, then the desert. Just give me a chance and I'll be back on my feet in no time and be able to do a bit of digging.'

'I'm sure you will,' James agreed, reaching for the discarded slippers and manoeuvring them carefully over the sore toes. He held out his hand. 'And good luck for tomorrow, Mr Carter. I look forward to seeing you pottering round the garden in a few months' time.'

'A few *months*? A few *weeks* is more like it,' the old man snorted as they moved away from his bedside.

CHAPTER TWO

KATE could smell the sea, mingling with the scent of pines and the wallflowers in the herbaceous borders, as soon as she stepped out of the main doors of the hospital that evening.

She stood on the steps and took a deep breath, drinking in the scented air and turning her face to the muted evening sunshine that was flooding the garden and driveway with soft golden light. The warmth was like a caress, the air like wine. This, she thought, is Millchester at its touristy best—sandy beaches, a sparkling sea dotted with sailing boats, warm spring sunshine and stately pine trees.

Wish-you-were-here sort of stuff, perfect for the holidaymakers who began to invade the small town from Easter onwards. Though, personally, she liked it just as well on grey, blustery, midwinter days, with the sea throwing up great plumes of spray against the wooden groynes. But, then, she was a native of Millchester and had grown up with the vagaries of the coastal weather.

She took another deep breath—it was good to be in the fresh air after being cooped up inside for hours. She walked slowly down the drive, unwinding after the busy, surprising day that had been triggered off by the unexpected arrival of James Bruce.

The dashing Dr Bruce, Meg Short had called him, but it was too flippant, too shallow a description of the big, solid, confident man with whom she had spent the morning.

He had hovered on the edge of her thoughts all the afternoon and even now as she ambled along at a snail's pace, enjoying her few minutes' solitude—a breathing space between work and home—she couldn't entirely dismiss him. He was still there, a large shadowy, masculine presence. Unexpectedly, her nostrils quivered. She could smell him, actually smell the acid tang of his aftershave, the scent of his soap, his essential maleness—it was almost as if he were walking beside her.

Bess must have seen her from the tiny casement window of her bedroom over the front porch for she came running up the drive to meet her, her long flaxen plait of hair swinging wildly from side to side.

Kate mentally blinked away the image of James Bruce.

God, I'm lucky, she thought as her daughter came hurtling toward her. My kids are super, so loving—they always seem really pleased to see me. I don't know what I've done to deserve them.

'Hi, Mum, you're late,' said Bess when she reached her. She linked her arm possessively through Kate's. At eleven, sturdy but leggy, she was nearly as tall as her mother. She beamed a smile at Kate, which was mirrored in the violet-blue eyes she'd inherited from her. 'I've put the casserole in the oven at three hundred and fifty, like you said in your note, and I've laid the table and the potatoes are ready to go on—and Philip's washing and topping the strawberries.'

'Strawberries! Where did they come from?' As if I don't know, she thought. Will my dear mother never stop spoiling us and, to be honest, do I really want her to?

'Granny brought them over from the nursery—they're the first out of the tunnel greenhouse. But she wouldn't stop—she and Gramps are busy. There are lots of visitors about already so they're keeping open late.'

Kate chuckled. 'Your grandparents are workaholics,' she said, a hint of admiration creeping into her voice.

'They should be thinking of retiring but they seem to be working harder than ever.'

'You're like them, Mum. You work jolly hard, too,' Bess relied, squeezing Kate's arm. 'I sometimes wish. . .' Her expressive eyes darkened.

'Wish what, Bess?'

'Well. . .that you didn't have to work so hard, just to sort of look after Philip and me. Do you mind, or do you sometimes wish that there was someone around to. . .?' Again her voice trailed off.

Kate stopped abruptly at the garden gate and turned a gently teasing face to her daughter. 'What, share the burden of bringing up you two monsters, Bess? Is that what you're trying to say, love?'

'Well, sort of.' Bess shrugged, and her cheeks flushed faintly. Then she mumbled in a rush, 'I mean, you don't want to get married again, or anything, do you?'

She looked at her daughter's solemn little face. It was a serious question, she realised, not to be brushed off lightly, but what sort of an answer is she expecting? What sort of answer should I give? The snappy answer would be—never again, once bitten twice shy.

But I can't do that, without giving her the wrong impression and putting her off marriage for good. How to explain that, because my marriage to her father was a disaster, not all relationships go wrong?

Yet she wants reassurance. She wants to know that I'm going to be around for her and Philip for ever. Someone's made her doubt that, and I've got to say the right thing and set her mind at rest.

She said carefully, trying to lighten the moment but not sound dismissive or facetious, 'Well, love, I've no plans for now, or in the foreseeable future, to get married or take a partner or whatever. I'm absolutely content and happy as I am. And, strange as it may seem. . .' she dropped a kiss on her daughter's cheek '. . .I don't consider either you or Philip a burden.'

Bess let out a little shriek of joy and her face lit up. 'Oh, Mum, I do love you.' She gave Kate a life-threatening hug. 'I knew you wouldn't do what Emma Porter's mum is going to do.'

As they reached the lodge and Kate opened her mouth to speak a car cruised down the drive from the direction of the hospital and the driver hooted at them. It was Grace, going off duty. They exchanged waves.

Kate unlatched the gate and pushed Bess through before her as another car turned into the drive from the coast road. Evening visiting had begun and the drive would be busy for an hour or so.

'And what is Mrs Porter going to do?' she asked, closing the gate behind them.

'Get married again, soon—though she's only just got divorced from Emma's dad—because she says she can't live without a man. And Emma doesn't like him and cried buckets at school because she misses her real dad. And I thought perhaps you felt like that, too, and would like to have a man around.'

'Well, I wouldn't like,' said Kate firmly, and then asked tentatively, 'Bess, do you or Philip ever miss your father?'

Bess looked astonished. 'Crumbs, no,' she said. 'We can hardly remember him—he was hardly ever at home, was he? He was a sort of stranger who came and went and always seemed to be angry about something. He wasn't very nice. I think the last time we saw him we were about five, and when you told us one day that you were getting divorced, and he wouldn't be coming home any more, we were glad.'

Kate said, making an effort to be honest but fair, 'He

wasn't a bad man, you know, just weak and unreliable, and he had a chip on his shoulder. He thought the world owed him a living but, of course, it didn't. Anyway, I'm glad you don't miss him, but if you ever want to get in touch with him we could try to track him down.'

She could have added that he was a mean, lazy, self-centred sponger who had used her *and*, what was worse, her parents as a meal ticket, and that he hadn't even wanted visiting rights to the twins when they'd parted. But, of course, she didn't.

'Oh, Mum, you are brilliant, but that's the last thing we'd want to do. You're all we want—you and Gran and Gramps.'

'Right, then, let's go in and see how the casserole's doing. I'm starving.'

Side by side they walked along brick path that led from the gate to the front door of the lodge, then circled round beneath the casement windows, framed with purple wistaria, to the back garden door.

The door, which led straight to the kitchen, stood wide open and the evening sunshine poured in across the gleaming quarry-tiled floor. Home sweet home, thought Kate happily as she and Bess paused in the doorway.

Philip, already several inches taller than both Bess and Kate, was bending over the cooker, fiddling with a dial and adjusting the lid of a saucepan. He lifted his head and his thick crown of hair—like Bess's, pale as flax, long on top and cropped at the back and sides in the presently favoured style—gleamed almost silver.

He gave them a wide grin. 'Hi, Mum. As you can see, I'm slaving away as usual while my sister goes bunking off.'

'Beast,' cried Bess indignantly. 'I peeled the potatoes and laid the table.'

'And I cleaned the carrots and the strawberries.'

'Hey, stop bickering, you two.' Kate said firmly, though she knew that they were not really bickering, only teasing each other. 'It's called division of labour. It's what we do in this house, and I'll do my share later and wash up and do some ironing while you two labour away at your homework project. Presumably you *have* made a start.'

'Almost finished—it was easy-peasy tonight.' They spoke in unison, as they so often did.

'So, what was it—this oh-so-easy project?'

'We had to pick out a report from today's news broadcasts and say why we thought it was important, in five hundred words or less. A current affairs project,' explained Philip. 'I went for an item on radio astronomy.'

That figures, thought Kate. He's always been a stargazer since he was a small boy. 'And what did you go for, Bess?'

'A piece about the Save the Children Fund, mainly about Mozambique—they're building medical centres and training health workers.'

That figured, too. Bess had wanted to be a nurse since she'd toddled around in a Red Cross outfit when she was three or thereabouts. And they both enjoyed writing, expressing themselves on paper. The project was tailor-made for them. No wonder they considered it a doddle.

Kate looked lovingly at their bright, intelligent young faces and thought, as she had earlier, how lucky she was to have such super kids.

'So,' she said, 'I think you both deserve supper and I know I do. Come on, I'll dish up. Let's eat.'

'And you can tell us all about your day,' said Bess, always eager for titbits of news about the hospital. 'Did anything exciting happen? Did you have any interesting cases in?'

'Well,' said Kate, 'the new medical director, Dr Bruce, turned up unexpectedly, and...' She launched into an edited description of the doctor and her busy morning.

Would one class it as an exciting day? wondered Kate a few hours later as she wallowed in a jasmine-scented bath. She closed her eyes and let her mind rove back over all that had happened.

It had been interesting, certainly, a breathless sort of day which had simply whizzed past. An up and down sort of day, and all of it due to the unexpected arrival of James Bruce that morning. A day of mixed emotions. From the moment she had met him in Grace's office until his departure just before lunch she had been acutely aware of his strong masculine presence. Strong but sensitive, a fascinating combination.

He'd come across as calm, rocklike, immensely reassuring.

She recalled how gently he had eased Mr Carter's outsize slippers on over his sore bunions when they had visited the surgical unit, and how comfortably he had chatted with tough old Dora Cross, striking exactly the right note in recognising her experience and professional expertise.

Was this the magical thing called charisma? Or was that too shallow an expression to use to describe the powerful vibes that emanated from him and of which she'd become increasingly conscious as the morning had worn on?

What a surprise he'd turned out to be, not in the least the sort of man she'd expected and dreaded. In a few hours he'd turned her thinking upside down, got under her defences. It was unbelievable, but she was actually looking forward to working with him. Of course, she wouldn't really know how well he would fit in until they were working together, but all the signs were that he would become part of the team, not just head of it. And she found herself fervently hoping it would be so.

He'd been brilliant on the round, friendly, pleasant, putting patients and staff at their ease but never patronising them. He hadn't overdone the charm but he certainly knew how to get along with people, all sorts of people, yet there was a slight air of reserve about him, and occasionally she'd glimpsed a shadowed expression in his hazel-green eyes.

He had nice eyes that crinkled at the corner when he smiled, and a nice mouth, too—well marked, well shaped but not thick, wide, generous. A mouth that would be nice to—

She came to with a jerk, splashing water over the side of the bath. It was getting cold. She shivered and turned on the hot tap with her big toe. What the hell was she thinking of, letting her mind wander like that? She wasn't interested in him as a man, only as a doctor, so it didn't matter a jot what his mouth was like.

So he'd impressed her, and though the whirlwind tour had completely disorganised her day, upsetting her plans to fit in some precious ward work, she hadn't minded.

It had been well worth missing out on direct nursing care for, having got off to a such a shaky start, the tour had turned out to be a cracking success and should pay future dividends.

He had wanted to see everything and she had been in her element, showing off each department—from the recently installed scanner and latest X-ray equipment to the small play group facilities and staff canteen.

It had pleased her immensely that he'd been as interested in the play group as in the scanner for she was equally proud of both, and both had required determination and effort to acquire.

'An absolute necessity, I would have thought,' he'd said as they stood in the doorway of the playroom and surveyed the roomful of noisy toddlers, 'with so many young women with children on the staff. But boards of trustees are not always prepared to acknowledge that something as mundane as a play facility is important. It's not as glitzy as a scanner. I guess someone did a lot of persuading.'

She recalled with a little frisson of pleasure the smile that he had slanted down at her, her eyes warm, knowing, gently teasing, and she had felt that he was reading her like a book.

'It was you, Kate, wasn't it? You railroaded them—or charmed them—into providing a play centre.' The Scottish burr in his soft, grainy voice had been very pronounced. Fascinating.

She had felt herself blushing slightly, and had nodded. 'With support from Grace. We pointed out that it would be virtually impossible to get enough part-time local help unless we had a child-minding centre, and we would have to bring in a lot of full-time outside staff and enlarge staff accommodation.'

'Which in the end would be more expensive *and* upset and locals who are responsible for most of the fund-raising,' he'd murmured. 'I like it—intelligent, oblique persuasion.'

'Precisely.'

Inordinately pleased that he'd understood so completely and obviously approved, she had smiled up at him. They had done a lot of smiling that morning, she thought now, which was strange considering the way things had started off between them.

They had by then been nearing the end of their tour, and his approval over the play group had further added to the surprising rapport that had sprung up between them as they had progressed round the hospital from department to department.

It had to be a good sign for the future, she mused, toeing the tap and releasing more hot water into the bath. She really must get out soon, but she'd stay just a few minutes longer. It was lovely lying here, mulling over all that had happened—so relaxing.

She heaved a sigh of contentment. All was right with her world—her children reassured, her hospital safe. James Bruce hadn't turned out to be the monster she had dreaded, but a sympathetic, knowledgeable professional with aims similar to her own.

And this had become even more obvious when they'd visited the operating theatre unit at the tail end of their tour.

This was immediately beneath the surgical ward and connected to it by its own service lift. The compact suite comprised an anteroom, operating theatre, recovery room, sterilising room and a stockroom.

'My word, very impressive for a single operating theatre. You're certainly well equipped,' the doctor had commented, peering into the stockroom which was crammed with an assortment of splints, packeted swabs and dressings, trays of instruments and a small blood refrigeration unit.

Sensing criticism, Kate had said defensively, 'We also supply the day surgical unit from here and they get through loads of stuff. They do masses of elective day ops.'

'Ah, of course, that makes sense since they're right next door, and their requirements are virtually the same as Theatre. A very practical arrangement.'

Once more there had been approval in his voice.

But as she and James had stood in the doorway of the theatre proper she'd been assailed by fresh doubts as to what his reaction would be to the cold, impersonal, nonfunctioning empty room. At that moment it had given the impression of being a wasted space, a lifeless place waiting for something to happen.

Tomorrow would be different, she'd thought. It would be bustling with green-gowned surgeons and nurses, going efficiently about their business in a sort of choreographed controlled chaos.

There would be technical equipment everywhere. The anaesthetic machine with its knobs and dials, and wires and cables snaking across the floor. Display screens would be lit up, and the gurgling suction machines would be guzzling up millilitres of blood which would otherwise obscure the surgeon's field of vision as he operated.

Would the perceptive Dr Bruce be able to picture it like that or would he just see it as it was today, a small underused theatre in a small provincial cottage hospital?

A lot of doctors were short on imagination, but she didn't think he was one of them. She wanted him to see it as she saw it—not as just a show place but as a workplace, and twice a week a busy workplace, functioning from early morning till late evening.

Knowing and loving the theatre as she did, as indeed she loved every part of the Memorial, it was easy for her to visualise it in action. But would this large, shrewd man, standing beside her, be able to visualise it, too? Could he see its potential? For some rather obscure reason, which she couldn't pin down, it was vitally important to her that he should see it as she saw it.

James had stood in silence, surveying the shining chrome and gleaming tiles, and Kate had held her breath. What would his verdict be?

After a few moments he'd said, 'Small but truly beautiful. Built for a purpose, a model operating theatre, state-of-the-art stuff. No wonder everyone's so proud of it. I'd have liked to have seen it on my last visit but it was in use, as indeed it should be.' He'd frowned, and turned his head sharply to look at Kate. 'Pity it isn't operating to full capacity. I always think that an empty theatre is a dead theatre—don't you agree?'

For a fraction of a second Kate bridled. Was he suggesting that the Memorial staff, doctors or nurses, weren't pulling their weight?

She met his eyes but couldn't read anything in their green and gold depths, and there was nothing in his expression to suggest that he was being critical. She rejected the idea—he was simply asking for an opinion, as one professional to another. He was putting into words what she herself had always thought.

For months she had been pleading for surgery at least three days a week, if not more. They had the facilities, they had—or could procure—the nursing staff, they certainly had the patients and, with the new six-bedded unit that had just been completed, they had the beds. But they were short of visiting surgeons.

The local GPs who operated on a rotational basis had originally planned to operate daily. But they were being stretched by the influx of newcomers into the new vast estate, creeping up the downs on the outskirts of the town, and now were reluctant to commit themselves to more surgery.

But James was absolutely right. An empty theatre *was* a dead theatre—a waste of space, a vacuum.

'I couldn't agree more,' she said firmly. 'We should have at least three lists a week, four even, but we simply haven't the surgical staff to man it and the board won't buy in more surgical help.'

He grinned. 'Well, you have now,' he said. 'Got a surgeon. I'm game. All we need is an anesthetist on a regular basis. And, surely, we could *sell* our services and bed and theatre space to the larger hospitals short of both—make it a viable proposition. That should please the trustees.' His eyes gleamed wickedly. 'What do you think, Kate, can we swing it? Will your friendly administrator back us up?'

His enthusiasm was infectious. It matched her own and she felt suddenly uplifted, almost light-headed.

'Let's give it a whirl,' she said with a little laugh. 'I'll speak to Grace about it tomorrow and set the ball rolling, though it'll take ages to get off the ground—these things always do. So it'll be up to you as medical director to use all your clout to convince the board.'

'We'll challenge them together, Kate.' He grinned. 'They won't won't know what's hit them. They won't be able to resist us—we'll make a formidable team.'

Kate grinned, too. 'You know, I rather think we will,' she agreed happily.

And what was left of his visit passed in a flash. They returned to the canteen and over coffee, consumed under the interested gaze of staff who came and went, exchanged snippets of information about themselves.

James wanted to know what had brought her to Millchester.

'Oh, I was born here,' she explained, 'and have lived and worked in this part of the world most of my life, except for a few years when I was training in London. That's why the Memorial means so much to me.' Then, avoiding any more questions, she asked quickly, 'And what about you—haven't you been recently working abroad with the World Health Organisation?'

'That's right,' he said tersely.

'Where?' she asked.

'Oh, recently in Africa, and before that a spell in the

former Yugoslavia, helping out in base and field hospitals and so on. I was with a detachment that had a sort of roving brief, not that we were allowed to rove anywhere much.' He sounded bitter.

Recalling the horrific pictures of wounded soldiers and civilians, she looked at him with frank admiration. 'That must have been pretty hairy.'

'Yep, it was at times. And trying to do what one could for the kids with ghastly injuries when we were short of water and painkillers, basic stuff, was frustrating to say the least.'

He took a sip of coffee and looked at her over the rim of the mug, his eyes sad and troubled. 'It's the children everywhere who get to you,' he said. 'The children and the sick and the elderly. They're so vulnerable, so helpless. And they've got so little and we've got so much.' He sounded almost accusing.

Frowning, Kate said, 'Are you saying that you think we have too much—here specifically?'

James frowned back at her. 'No,' he said firmly, 'I'm not saying that at all, but what I *am* saying is that we mustn't waste what we've got. We owe it to this community to give them the best health care ever.'

The expression in his eyes changed to one of brightness and alertness. He put down his coffee and, stretching over the table, lightly touched the backs of her hands as they clasped her mug. 'We must never forget that the hospital's here to serve *them*, Kate, and it'll be up to you and me as head of nursing and head of medicine to see that it does.'

He leaned back in his chair and chuckled. A grainy chuckle, she thought, to match his voice. 'But, then, who am I to preach to the converted? As I said before, Kate, we're going to make a great team.' For a moment his eyes met and locked with hers in mutual understanding, then he looked at his watch, swallowed the last of his coffee and stood up. 'I've an appointment to keep,' he said abruptly. 'Thanks for the tour. I've enjoyed every moment of it. See you next week.'

Kate opened her mouth to speak, but with a wave of his hand he turned on his heel and strode out of the canteen.

'And goodbye to you too, partner,' Kate muttered to his retreating back.

But only now, as she lay in the cooling water of the bath, going over the events of the day, did Kate realise the significance of what she had done. She, who had dreaded the thought of the new man making changes, had conspired with him to do just that. She had jumped at the chance of doing what she had been urging the board to do for months—extend the operating list, a project dear to her heart.

What an irony that the man she had seen as the enemy should be her fellow conspirator. But, as he'd said, when it came to matters medical they were on the same wavelength.

Grace would laugh like a drain at her U-turn, she thought wryly, but, what the hell, it was an immensely comforting feeling to know that the new director was on her side. She still wasn't sure of him as a man but as a doctor, as a partner working beside her to make the Memorial a small but perfect centre of medical excellence, he looked like being the tops.

Shivering, she scrambled out of the bath and wrapped herself in a huge soft towel. But *what* was he like as a man? she wondered. He seemed warm and friendly and had nice eyes, kind eyes that had been full of compassion when he'd spoken of the injured children he'd met up with when he was with the WHO. And he'd understood so well about providing care for the staff children. He certainly seemed to be a perceptive, sensitive man.

He probably had a family of his own—smaller versions of himself, with dark brown hair and hazel eyes—presided over by a tall, stunning-looking woman who ran his home like clockwork.

The idea brought her up with a jerk. What on earth had put that notion into her head? It was just as likely, perhaps even more likely considering the fact that he'd been working abroad, that he was unattached, a free agent.

Not that it mattered two hoots, she thought, pulling on her knee-length sloppy nightshirt. She knew nothing about him personally and he knew precious little about her, and that was fine. All that was important was that they formed and maintained a close working partnership.

And on that thought she took herself off to bed and slept soundly till the pigeons, burbling in the fir tree that stood sentinel over the lodge, woke her at six as usual.

Grace didn't hoot with laughter, as Kate had expected that she might, when they met for mid-morning coffee and she admitted that James Bruce was not the ogre that she had feared. But she did raise astonished eyebrows when Kate explained that they planned to approach the board about opening up the theatre for one or more extra sessions a week, and wanted her support.

'Well, I have to admire you, Kate,' she said. 'You haven't lost any time lobbying for this project which you've been pestering everyone about for months. But I'm surprised you've won our new man over so quickly. He doesn't strike me as easy to manipulate, even for you.'

'Oh, I didn't have to do any lobbying, and I certainly didn't do any manipulating. James put forward the idea himself. Like me, he thinks that the theatre is a waste of space unless it's used to capacity. And once we get it off the ground we can make it pay for itself by selling our services to other hospitals.'

Grace said dryly, 'The finance people and the board will like that, and of course it's up to him as Director if he wants to spend much of his valuable time doing surgery—he'd got a free hand.'

'So you'll support us if it comes to the crunch?'

'You know me, Kate. I'll support anything that furthers patient care if it's a viable proposition. It'll be up to you prove that you can supply nursing cover as necessary, and that Dora Cross and the surgical nursing staff are one hundred per cent behind you since they'll bear the brunt of an extra operating list.'

'You know Dora—she'll jump at the chance. She hates having empty beds and likes to keep her staff on their toes. Well, you know her motto—a busy nurse is a happy nurse. She's an old-fashioned dragon of a ward sister but her staff think the world of her and they'll be behind her all the way.'

'How did she get on with our Dr Bruce? Did she approve?'

Kate giggled. 'She grilled him a bit but he bowled her over. You might say that they parted on terms of mutual admiration.'

'From what I hear,' Grace said, quirking her lips in a wry smile, 'that gentleman's bowled everyone over, including you and me, eh, Kate? He's certainly a charmer, but there's nothing shallow about him. I believe we've hooked ourselves a dedicated doctor and a thoroughly nice man. I was very impressed and I'm looking forward to working with him.'

'Yes,' said Kate, with surprising fervour, 'so am I.'

CHAPTER THREE

FOR Kate the next few days were, as always, busy, yet busy as she was, moving briskly from one job to the next, she found herself thinking frequently of James Bruce. Too frequently, she thought guiltily, trying to squash his image. The wretched man seemed to have taken up lodgings in her subconscious, popping to the fore from time to time and almost, but not quite, distracting her from her work.

She was in a maelstrom of mixed emotions. Part of her was looking forward to his arrival on Monday whilst part of her was apprehensive, but one thing was sure—she couldn't get him out of her mind. Even at the weekend when she was off duty—going about her domestic chores, pottering in the garden, shopping with the twins, and visiting her parents at their fruit and flower nurseries—she found herself thinking about him.

In fact, on Sunday evening, while she was playing a hilarious, haphazard game of croquet on the uneven lawn at the back of the cottage with Philip and Bess, Philip had accused her of being, 'off the planet'. 'Hey, come back to earth, Mum,' he said, as she stood staring down at the ball she was supposed to strike.

Irritated that James had even invaded her precious time with her children, she shoved away the vivid image of the doctor and whacked the ball with such force that she drove it through two hoops.

So it was strange, considering how much James had been in her thoughts, that she was so surprised to see him when she arrived early for work on Monday morning. But she *was* surprised, and she came to an abrupt halt when she rounded the corner of the corridor and found him leaning nonchalantly against the wall beside her office door.

He heaved himself away from the wall and gave her a beaming smile. 'Hello,' he said, in his rich, grainy voice. 'Lovely morning.'

To her astonishment and chagrin, her heart did a curious little flip at the sight of him. He looked casually elegant in narrow cavalry twill trousers that flattered his long legs and a lightweight, tweedy jacket tailored to fit his broad shoulders, worn over a gleaming white shirt and a tastefully jazzy tie.

Kate, rattled by the wave of pleasure washing over her, ignored his greeting. 'You're early,' she said accusingly.

His eyes twinkled as his smile broadened. 'Like you, I'm an early bird.'

'Out to catch the unsuspecting worm?' Her voice came out sharp, scathing.

Immediately the smile disappeared, as did the twinkle in his hazel eyes. 'Accusing me of spying on your precious staff, Sister?' he asked in a silky voice. 'Because I can assure you that nothing was further from my mind. I don't do that sort of thing—I like everything up front when dealing with my colleagues.'

Kate felt her cheeks flame—for a brief moment that was precisely what she had thought—that he was there to surreptitiously check out the night staff. But already she was regretting the thought. All her instincts told her that he just wouldn't stoop to do such a thing.

No wonder he was offended. Why the hell had she implied such a thing? She must find the words to put things right. Nothing must interfere with the rapport that they'd established on Wednesday. Their future working relationship depended on it.

Her mind raced. She must be frank with him. She said softly, 'No, Dr Bruce, I don't think you would spy, as you put it. Though, to be truthful, it did flash across my mind for a second that you were making a surreptitious recce, but it was gone in an instant. It was just that you surprised me by being here so early, and I was reminded of the old saying about the early bird catching the worm.' She stepped forward and held out her hand. 'I'm sorry if I offended you.'

He looked at her in silence for a moment, then extended his hand and clasped hers. 'We seem to make a habit of this,' he said, the hard line of his lips relaxing a little, 'being rude and then apologising. We keep wrong-footing each other.'

'Let's hope this will be the last time,' Kate replied as they shook hands.

He grinned then and his eyes twinkled again. 'I doubt it, for although we both want what's best for the Memorial we're not always going to agree on how to go about it, at least not until you learn to trust me more.'

Kate breathed in sharply. 'But I do trust you.'

James Bruce shook his head. 'No, you don't—not entirely. But why should you? You don't know me. You don't resent me as you did when we first met, but you still feel over-protective about your staff—about the hospital as a whole. Part of you hopes that we'll work well together, but part of you is still wary of me.'

She opened her mouth to protest again, but thought better of it. He was spot on. She was looking forward to working with him but she was also still a little chary of sharing her professional responsibilities with him, in spite of what he'd said about them forming a good partnership.

Taking a deep breath, she said softly, 'You're dead right. I've been handling things on my own for so long that I'm a bit scared of any change. Look, let's go into my room and I'll try to explain.' She took a key out of her jacket pocket and stepped forward to her office door.

James whisked the key out of her fingers. 'Allow me,' he said, smoothly unlocking the door and pushing it open.

'Thank you,' she murmured as she slipped past him, catching a whiff of tweedy scent and musky soap as she brushed against his broad chest.

She took off her jacket, sat down behind her desk and motioned him to take one of the chairs opposite.

He took his seat and crossed one long leg over the other, looking totally relaxed. 'You don't have to explain, you know,' he said mildly. 'Just let's give ourselves a bit of space, a bit of time to work things out.'

Kate was positive. 'But I *want* you to understand. You see, your predecessor, dear old Dr Mac, was a senior GP who'd been one of the prime movers in getting this place off the ground. He passionately believed that each community should have its own small hospital, built by the community for the community. He would have played an active role in it, but by the time it was opened his heart was a bit dodgy and he was appointed medical director with no specific duties, except to be here.'

'In other words, he was virtually a sleeping partner, leaving the management of the place to you and Grace Lyons.'

'Yes, not that we minded. He was a poppet and always there with advice if we needed it, and there were enough visiting GPs to provide bedside medical care initially. But they've been under pressure since the new housing estate was built, and they're finding it difficult to cover here and their practices. It was inevitable that a more active medical director would be appointed.'

'And then your nice old Dr Mac had a coronary and I popped out of the woodwork, considerably younger and more active, posing a threat to the established order of things. And you were all geared to resist me, weren't you, Kate?'

He leaned forward and put his elbows on the desk, supporting his chin on his clasped hands. His face was on a level with hers, and Kate found herself looking directly into his kindly and amused hazel-green eyes.

'But it didn't work out like that, did it?' he continued softly. 'I wasn't quite the ogre you'd expected. I was willing to be co-operative, openly admired the way you were running your beloved hospital and that threw you. Oh, Kate, I'm not surprised—'

The telephone rang. Kate blinked herself free of his mesmerising eyes and reached out for the phone. 'Yes, Dr Bruce is here,' she said briskly, after listening for a moment. 'I'll tell him.' She replaced the receiver.

'That was Neil Peters, the young learner GP who was on resident call duty last night. He was ringing from Reception to ask if he may have a word with you, before reporting off.'

James stood up, looking large and formidable. 'He most certainly may. I would expect nothing less—he's got to hand over to me officially.' Frowning, he looked down at Kate. 'Surely that's the drill—to provide continuous medical cover?'

'Yes, but it doesn't have to be to the director if he happens not to be here to take over when the night medic is ready to leave. He can hand over to the first day doctor to come on duty, whether it's the radiologist or a GP doing a round of his patients. And in addition there's a rota of on-call doctors who live nearby and can be here within minutes.' His frown deepened, and she said sharply, 'We've never had any problems—it works well.'

A mocking smile replaced the frown. 'On the defensive again, Sister Brown,' he said in a dry-as-dust voice as he strode to the door. 'Will you phone Reception and ask Dr Peters to come to my office, stat?'

'Certainly, Dr Bruce,' she said, with all the calm she could muster as he disappeared into the corridor. And then she added to the empty room, 'Damn, damn, damn the man.'

She was still tight-lipped and frowning ferociously a few minutes later when the night sister, June Brookes, tall and majestic, sailed into the office.

'You look rattled, Kate,' she said in her direct fashion. 'What's wrong, old thing?'

'Our new medical director, making snide remarks, that's what's wrong. He's conceited and patronising and—'

'Really? I thought he seemed intelligent and courteous and not the sort to throw his weight about. It may be an old-fashioned notion but I think good manners are important, and he's certainly got them.'

'Veneer,' Kate snorted. Then she said in surprise, 'How do you know what he's like? When did you meet him?'

'This morning. Quite properly he got the night porter to track me down and introduced himself when he arrived.'

Kate smothered a groan. 'He didn't say and I practically accused him of sneaking in.'

'Well, you were wide of the mark there. Friendly and laid-back he may be, but I guess he's a stickler for professional etiquette,' said June. She glanced at her fob watch, resting on her ample bosom. 'Now, shall I give you a run-down on last night?'

'Please.'

It didn't take long for June to deliver her verbal report—there would be more details on the wards.

There had been two admissions during the night, both seen by Dr Peters.

Miss Stephanie Pye, aged thirty, had been admitted to the women's medical wing with severe abdominal pain—query an infection of the colon or a possible grumbling appendix, or—It was open ended, awaiting further diagnosis. An injection of codeine had been given to relieve the pain, and she had been put on a fluids-only diet pro tem. Blood pressure, pulse and respiration within normal limits, temperature a little high.

The second admission was to Men's Medical, a Mr Lawrence North, aged eighty, who'd had a stroke. He had a left-side hemiplegia, some slurring of speech, was conscious and *compos mentis* though a little restless. Dr Peters had prescribed a mild sedative, diazepam, given by injection. Patient made comfortable and sleeping at time of report.

'There's not a lot else,' said June. 'Usual sort of night. Mrs Pickford had an asthma attack, not severe, responded to reassurance, prescribed medication and a cup of tea. Karen White, the young rheumatic, had a lot of pain and discomfort. Joints massaged with analgesic cream and prescribed anti-inflammatory painkiller given, with minimal effect.'

She paused, looking up from her notes. 'You know, Kate, I think that young woman should have her case reviewed. She's eighteen, for God's sake, and crippled, poor kid, and she's still on the same medication she was on when she was last admitted. Let's hope our new medicine man can do something about it. In fact, I hope Dr Bruce will check up on all the bods I've mentioned in report. With luck, he'll come up with some answers.'

'Yes, I think he might,' Kate said rather reluctantly. 'The GPs seem to think highly of him and have given him carte blanche to take over in-patient treatment management. I know some of them are looking forward to being less involved.'

June stood up. 'And quite right, too. Old Dr Mac was a dear but, let's face it, you and Grace propped him up from day one. He wasn't much practical use to anyone.' She began to walk towards the door. 'I know it's going to be tough for you at first, Kate, sharing the load, but the load's getting heavier and change is in the air. Give our Dr Bruce a chance. Trust him, I think he's going to turn out to be first class. . . He's got good hands,' she added, apropos of nothing in particular.

A little later, watching and listening to him as he reassured a nervous Stephanie Pye, Kate found herself agreeing with June's assessment of James Bruce. He showed all the signs of being the sort of doctor she most admired, asking searching questions and actually listening to what the patient had to say in reply until he had obtained a comprehensive medical history.

June was right. He *was* to be trusted, and the fact that she unexpectedly, and temporarily, she told herself fiercely, found herself disturbed by him as a man must not be allowed to cloud her professional judgement.

And he *had* got good hands—longish fingers with square tips—competent hands, she thought as he began his examination. She had liked his easy yet professional manner with the patients when they had done the round together on Wednesday, but now, seeing him at work, it was crystal clear that there was more to him than just smooth bedside manners.

It was quite obvious that he was very experienced as he

confidently, gently and methodically pressed and palpated the patient's tender abdomen and listened through his stethoscope for bowel sounds. He went over the whole abdomen thoroughly, but returned finally to the right side, pressing carefully from groin to waist and down again.

He's looking for something else, not an inflamed appendix, thought Kate as he slid one hand beneath the patient's back and with the other lightly finger-kneaded high over the pelvic area.

Stephanie Pye gasped and widened big brown eyes. 'Hell, that hurt.'

The doctor straightened up. 'Sorry about that—all finished now,' he said. 'Ordeal over.'

He stood back while Kate tidied the bedclothes and gave the young woman a sip of water, then he sat down on the edge of bed and took her hand for a moment.

Her eyes were frightened. 'They told me I might have a grumbling appendix and it might be inflamed. Is it going to burst?'

He shook his head and squeezed her hand. 'No, Miss Pye, it isn't,' he said decisively, 'because I'm pretty sure you haven't got a grumbling appendix, inflamed or otherwise.'

'Oh, what a relief. I thought I might get peritonitis or something really scary. I had a cousin who died from a perforated appendix. But if it's not my appendix, Doctor, what is wrong with me—what's giving me all this pain?'

'From what you've told me about your recent heavy, painful and erratic periods, I believe you have something called salpingitis—that's inflammation of the Fallopian tubes, caused by infection.'

Now why didn't Neil Peters suss that out as a possible? wondered Kate.

Stephanie Pye wondered, too, and asked a trifle belligerently, 'Why didn't the doctor who saw me last night suspect that?'

James said quietly, 'Because the signs were all low down on the right side of your abdomen, similar to those indicating an inflamed appendix or some colonic infection, and disguised the infection of a single Fallopian tube when usually both tubes are affected.'

'So, how come you diagnosed it, Doctor?'

Yes, how did you, Kate thought, and how will you explain, without making young Peters look a fool?

Fleetingly James caught Kate's questioning eye and gave her a sardonic little half-smile. He knew exactly what she was thinking.

'Because I'm an old hand and lucky enough to have come across this before. Dr Peters is qualified, has done his hospital training but is only just beginning to gain practical experience as a general practitioner. I'm sure you can appreciate that—you're a teacher and you know there's a vast difference between a newly qualified and an experienced teacher. Well, it's the same in medicine. We learn as we go along, and we never stop learning.'

Like it, thought Kate. Nice way of putting it to give Neil a face saver—decent of him. She felt a little surge of pleasure at the thought, which she immediately squashed. Most doctors would have done the same to cover for a colleague.

Miss Pye said slowly, 'That's true. Thank you for explaining. Now, can you please tell me how you're going to treat this salpingitis?'

'Today we'll do some blood tests, take a vaginal swab and start you on an antibiotic. I want you to take in plenty of fluids, and rest. Tomorrow I want to do a laparoscopy—that's an internal examination under anaesthetic to confirm the extent and possible cause of the infection. I'll be in to see you after that to have a chat. And don't worry, Miss Pye—we'll get you sorted out.'

He patted her hand again and then, with a nod and a calm, reassuring smile, he left he cubicle. After making sure that the patient was comfortable and had a glass of water to hand, Kate followed him.

He was thoughtful as they walked side by side to the nurses' station. 'Do we have any info about whether our Stephanie has a regular partner?' he asked, with a sideways glance at Kate.

Kate shook her head. 'There's nothing on the admission sheet and there was no one with her when she was admitted. She gives her next of kin as her parents, who live in Guernsey. Why, is it important?'

'Well, she's on the Pill, but was a bit cagey about discussing it. She doesn't strike me as the sort of woman who plays the field so the chances of a sexually transmitted infection is low, though not impossible. And though occasionally salpingitis is transmitted through a blood-borne infection such as tuberculosis there's nothing in her history to suggest that. So what are we left with?'

Was James testing her or did he want an opinion?

'Infection following childbirth, or—'

'Spontaneous or induced abortion. Well, clearly she's not given birth, which leaves us with abortion as the most likely cause. Very early abortion. There were no obvious exterior signs of pregnancy when I examined her abdomen and no detectable breast changes.'

They reached the station, which was at that moment unmanned, and he perched himself on a high stool behind the desk. He patted the stool beside him and Kate hitched herself up onto it, resting her feet on the crossbar. They sat sideways to the desk.

He didn't speak for a moment but stared down at his

stethoscope, running the length of it through his fingers. Then abruptly he lifted his head and frowned at Kate. 'So, we're most likely talking about a spontaneous abortion. She wouldn't have had time for a planned one...unless, of course, it was self-induced and that was why she was being so cagey. What do you think, Kate? What does your woman's intuition tell you?'

So it was Kate again—very friendly. He leaned forward until their knees were nearly touching. She wished he wouldn't look at her so hard with those clear hazel-green eyes that seemed to see so much—so often amused but now serious. And she wished, too, that she wasn't so aware of his nearness, his masculine presence. It was ridiculous and downright disconcerting.

Blow him! She would not allow herself to be attracted to the man, however charismatic he was. She was prepared to admire him as a doctor, but that was it. Fiercely, she repeated her usual mantra in her head—men as men I can do without.

Kate returned his stare and said in a dry voice, 'I don't know about intuition, but it's obvious that Miss Pye's an intelligent woman. If she suspected that she was pregnant she wouldn't take any risk. She would go and see her doctor and get it sorted out properly. I think it's much more likely that with her erratic periods the idea didn't cross her mind and she's had a spontaneous abortion.'

James nodded. 'Yep, you're probably right. Now, if I can have her file I'll write up her notes and medication and leave you to organise her nursing care. I must go back to my office for a while and then, if I may, I'll come back to have a look at the other new admission and the rheumatic girl you mentioned.'

'Right, Doctor.' She kept her voice flat and expressionless.

'Of course, if you're too busy you don't have to escort me. One of the staff nurses, perhaps...'

Was he being sarcastic or thoughtful? Play it cool, she reminded herself.

'I'm covering for Ward Sister so, of course, I'll escort you. It's an old-fashioned rule of the house that senior doctors are accompanied by the senior nurse on duty,' she said primly. He could scarcely quarrel with that since he was hot on protocol.

The amused gleam was back in his eyes.

'Fair enough. I wouldn't dream of breaking the rules—bending them occasionally perhaps if the situation dictates but not breaking them for the sake of doing so. I've found that most rules have a basis in common sense, as I'm sure this one has.'

His voice ended on a note of enquiry, or was it irony?

'It certainly has,' said Kate, her voice tart. 'It's to enable the doctor to pass on any instructions direct to whoever's responsible for seeing that they're carried out—in this instance, me. It ensures continuity of patient care.'

'In other words, chain of command—the buck stops here.'

'Precisely.'

'You're quite right, it makes good sense. It's a good rule. I shouldn't have questioned it. You know exactly what you're about where your patients' welfare is concerned, Kate.' It was a statement of fact, not an empty compliment.

His eyes crinkled at the corners, he smiled and she found herself smiling back.

So much for playing it cool, she thought ruefully after he'd left the ward and she was back in the ward office. It seemed James had only to smile and all her good intentions dissolved. She hadn't meant to be charmed, but he was charming her just as he had charmed Grace and the formidable Dora Cross and plain-speaking June Brookes.

They had all seen that there was more to the man than just his charm, and she could see that, too, so why was she bothered—why did she feel that she had to resist his friendly advances?

Obviously, because she knew she mustn't allow herself to fall under his spell and be manipulated. For, in spite of all his assurances that he had no intention of trying to take over control, she still had some reservations.

Who are you kidding? whispered a voice deep inside her head. Be honest, you're not afraid of him in his role as Director—you're afraid of being attracted to him as a man if you let him get under your skin. And he's already started to do that, whispered the same voice.

She buried herself in paperwork, but the thought was still nagging away at her when he returned to the ward half an hour later to examine Mr North, the newly admitted stroke case, and Karen White, the rheumatoid arthritis patient.

He was as impressive with them as he had been with Stephanie Pye, asking questions and patiently listening to the answers. And it had required a great deal of patience to make sense of Lawrence North's slurred speech. But he had persisted, got a potted history from him and succeeded in establishing a rapport by explaining to him the nature of his stroke and outlining his future treatment.

'The aim is to get you mobile as soon as possible,' he told the elderly gentleman, sitting on the side of the bed and gently massaging the thin, useless hand as he spoke. 'I'm going to arrange for the physiotherapist to give you exercises twice a day—nothing too strenuous to start with, but building up to restore movement to your arm and leg.

This should be possible as you appear to have had only a slight stroke, which we will confirm by giving you a brain scan.'

Mr North struggled to speak, touching his slack lips with his good hand.

Apparently understanding him, James said, 'You're wondering if your speech will return to normal?'

Mr North nodded slowly.

'Yes, there's an excellent chance that it will, with help from the speech therapist. She'll visit to help you with your swallowing and enable you to recover your normal speech pattern as soon as possible. But, as with the physiotherapy, you'll have to co-operate—convalescence is hard work, old chap.'

The slack mouth contorted into the semblance of a smile, and the single word, 'Try,' bubbled out as James and Kate moved away from the bed.

Kate said impulsively as they made their way to the women's wing of the ward, 'You were great with old Mr North—so patient. Stroke cases, especially where speech is affected, are so difficult to examine that it's easy to give up on them. A lot of doctors do. But you didn't and you actually got a response from him. I was very impressed.'

James came to an abrupt halt in the middle of the corridor that divided the women's ward from the men's, a sort of no man's land. He laid a detaining hand on Kate's arm. The pressure of his hand was unnerving. She half turned and he swung to face her. His eyes were twinkling brightly. Clearly he was very amused.

'Do you mean to say, Kate, that you actually approve, without reservation, of something that I've done?'

Kate stared at him in astonishment. 'I. . .I don't know what you mean,' she faltered, as she felt her cheeks reddening. 'I don't know why you should be so surprised by a well-deserved compliment.'

'Don't you, Kate?'

She shook her head and blurted out, 'No. So why are you?'

James gave an exaggerated sigh and pulled a whimsical face. 'Because I've done very little this morning that seemed to please you, starting with turning up too early.'

Kate made a little negative gesture with her hands. 'But I apologised for reacting over that.'

'And then went into defence mode a few minutes later over another trivial point which you saw as a slight to the hospital.' Suddenly he was serious, his eyes grave. 'What is it Kate? What's bugging you about me—why are you giving me such a hard time? I thought after the understanding we reached on Wednesday and our talk this morning that you had accepted me—wanted me as a colleague—but it seems I was wrong and you still resent my presence here.'

'No, I don't.' She was vehement. 'I think you're just the sort of doctor we need, but. . .' Her voice trailed off. What could she say? *I find you too attractive as a man and that scares me? I don't want a man in my life—I've got my lovely children, my job and I don't want any complications and men mean complications?*

Of course she couldn't say any of these things. He'd think she was mad, especially as he wasn't suggesting anything but an amicable working relationship and she was into the realms of romantic fantasy.

'I can't explain it,' she said abruptly. 'I'm sorry.'

James peered into her lovely, puzzled, violet-blue eyes and his heartbeat quickened. He hadn't a clue why she was so uptight, but he was desperately keen to reassure her. Damsel in distress, he thought cynically. White knight to the rescue.

In his soft, deep, grainy voice, he said, 'Then don't try to explain. As I said earlier, we've bags of time to get to know each other properly. And bear with me if I sometimes criticise. I'm not trying to catch you out—I simply want to know what makes things tick. I'm here to support you, not undermine you, Kate.' He bent his head so that his face was only inches from hers, and said with unexpected fierceness, 'You've got to believe that, my dear Sister Brown.'

His mouth was so close that Kate thought for one wild moment that he was going to kiss her. She took an instinctive step backwards and immediately regretted it. It was a dead give-away—surely a man of his perceptiveness would now know exactly what she'd been thinking. Mentally she squirmed. How damned humiliating. She must squash that idea—make light of it.

Willing herself not to blush, she said without a tremor, even conjuring up a smile of sorts, 'Of course I believe you, James. Sorry if I've been, to say the least, rather prickly. Thanks for being so understanding and patient.' Her smile widened and she made a tremendous effort to appear relaxed. 'Promise I'll do better in the future,' she added gaily.

Casually he reached out a hand and lightly touched her cheek in a natural, almost avuncular fashion. 'You will,' he said confidently. 'We're going to make a brilliant team, you and I.'

His eyes held a tender, amused gleam as they met hers for an instant.

His touch was electric and her cheek tingled—but, thank God, he couldn't see that. 'So you said once before,' she reminded him dryly, somehow keeping her voice steady and ignoring the gleam in his eyes, 'when we did our tour on Wednesday.'

'So I did,' replied James cheerfully, 'because it happens to be true and, as the pundits say, truth will out.' And with that somewhat enigmatic remark, he began striding across the corridor toward the women's ward. 'Now, Sister, shall we get on and take a look at Karen White?' he said.

As if the last few minutes' intimate conversation hadn't taken place, thought Kate irritably as she hurried after him.

CHAPTER FOUR

ONLY long practice made it possible for Kate to put all thoughts of this emotive conversation out of her mind as she joined James at Karen White's bedside.

As she'd expected, he was as thorough, gentle and reassuring with Karen as he had been with Lawrence North and Stephanie Pye, but in a slightly more casual fashion as befitted her youth.

He doesn't miss a trick, Kate thought admiringly, listening to him as he enthusiastically discussed the relative merits of current pop groups with the young woman, getting on to her wavelength, to put her at ease as he examined her.

Gently he ran his fingers over her inflamed and swollen joints, flexing and extending them just enough to establish their range of movement.

At the end of his examination he sat down on the edge of her bed and, with the frankness that Kate was recognising as his hallmark, spelt out her future treatment. 'We're going to try you on a different non-steroid anti-inflammatory drug, Karen, and a stronger painkiller,' he explained.

Karen pulled a face, which he acknowledged with a slight smile as he continued, 'And we'll start you on an anti-rheumatic drug. This will hopefully slow down the course of the disease so that you maintain your current ability, which normally isn't bad, and perhaps even improve it. But it's *not* a miracle cure and will take a while to work. It's not going to do anything for you immediately.'

'Well, surprise, surprise,' muttered Karen sarcastically.

James was gently, 'I didn't say it wouldn't work, love. But while you're suffering this acute attack I want you to keep warm and rest in bed, and with bed rest and your much stronger medicine you'll quickly begin to improve.'

'But I'll get stiffer and stiffer and won't be able to walk at all—it always happens if I have to stay in bed. It takes me weeks to get back on my feet,' Karen wailed.

'Well, it won't happen this time, I promise. I'll arrange for you to have daily physio and massage, which will keep your muscles toned, and I guarantee you won't stiffen up. Come on, give it a whirl, Karen—you've nothing to lose, have you?'

Karen shrugged. 'OK, I suppose. I'll give it a go, if you say it'll help,' she said, batting spiky eyelashes heavy with mascara at James. In spite of the make-up, she looked more like a brash sixteen-year-old than eighteen, thought Kate. 'But can't I get up at all?' she asked plaintively. 'Not even when my boyfriend comes?'

'Not a chance,' said James. 'You need complete bed rest.'

'Couldn't we just go into the lounge and watch the telly! It's dead boring in here, with everyone always watching us.'

James shook his head. 'Nope, not for a few days,' he said firmly. 'It's tough, I know, love, but give your new medication a chance to work. Stick to the rules now and you could be joining in your local rave-up in a few months' time.'

Her pinched little elfin face lit up. 'Is that a promise?'

'No, not a promise but a possibility—something to aim for if you co-operate with your new treatment. Once this acute flare-up had died down you'll be doing increased daily exercises, including swimming, to get you properly mobile. It'll take patience and hard work and courage, but it'll be worth it, believe me.' He stood up and asked. 'How old's your boyfriend, Karen?'

'Stevie? He's eighteen, same as me. We've been going out together since we were kids—we were at school together. S'pose we'll get married one day, that's if I don't get any worse. Dunno whether he'll stick with me if I do.' Her eyes glistened with sudden tears.

She looked young and terribly vulnerable and Kate wanted to hug her but, that not being possible, she smoothed the tangle of black hair away from the girl's forehead and said firmly, 'We're going to do all we can to see that that doesn't happen, Karen. That's why Dr Bruce is putting you on this new top-of-the-range medication. You're in with a real chance of more than holding your own if you stick with it and do as he says.'

Karen grabbed Kate's hand. 'Do you really think so?' she asked, her eyes pleading for further reassurance.

'Yes, I really do. You're in safe hands with Dr Bruce, believe me, he really does know his stuff. Trust him—if anyone can, he'll get you well.' To avoid meeting James's eyes, after paying him such a fulsome compliment, she busied herself and started to tidy the bedclothes and plump up the pillows.

'Well, thank you, Sister, for your vote of confidence. Now I'm sure of Karen's co-operation.' James said in a cool voice, and then added in a much warmer one to Karen, 'Your Stevie sounds a nice caring sort of chap—what say we get him involved in helping you with your exercises? Would he go along with that, do you think?'

Her eyes shone. 'He might if you talked to him.'

'When's he due in to see you?'

'This evening.'

'Right, I'll drop by about half past seven.'

'Thanks, Doctor, you're brilliant.'

James smiled his fascinating, eye-crinkling smile and, with a wave of his hand, turned and strode briskly toward the door.

But when Kate joined him a few minutes later in Ward Sister's office he wasn't smiling—he was reading Karen's file and looking grim.

'What the hell does this child's GP think he's doing?' he muttered savagely through tight lips. 'She's been on her present drug regime since she was first diagnosed a couple of years ago, apparently without it being reviewed. And she hasn't had any physio or other constructive treatment. No wonder she's had a second flare-up in a year. And she was in here for a week a few months ago so why the hell didn't you persuade your precious Dr Mac do something about it, Sister?'

His usually kind hazel eyes were cold and hard, glittering with little gold sparks as they met hers. His face was a rigid mask of fury.

Cool it, thought Kate, squashing the desire to make a sharp retort. I mustn't mind him taking it out on me—it's only because he cares so much for his patient.

She said quietly, 'Her GP wouldn't agree to any change of medication—just wanted her nursed through the acute period with bed rest. There was nothing Dr Mac could do though he tried hard to make Karen's doctor change his mind, especially about the analgesics. And I did my level best to persuade him, too, believe me, but. . .'

'But?'

'But he flatly refused—said that he didn't believe in prescribing stronger painkillers at this stage in an ongoing chronic condition. Well, he had a point—as you know, some doctors do hold that view. He insisted that she was his patient, he just wanted her to have nursing care and he would not hand over management control to Dr Mac.'

'But I've got it now, have I not—full control?'

'Yes. Karen was sent in by another member of the partnership who specifically asked that you should take over.'

His grim mouth relaxed a little. 'So no one's going to fight me over the new regime I've suggested?'

'No one.'

'Just as well.' His voice was crisp. 'They would have had a hell of a battle on their hands.' He stared hard at Kate for a moment. 'Would you have supported me if there had been a battle?'

'Certainly I would. No way would I have allowed a repeat of the previous episode. I would have supported you all the way to the top,' she said firmly, unflinchingly meeting his hard-eyed stare with one of her own.

He turned abruptly and looked out of the window for a moment, and when he turned back his eyes had lost their hardness and his voice its crispness. He said almost diffidently, 'Sorry about making that snide remark about you and your Dr Mac. It was quite uncalled-for.'

The remnants of her simmering anger died. She shrugged and made her voice dry, though she would have liked to have given him a comforting hug just as she had wanted to give little Karen a hug for he, too, in spite of his size and air of authority looked vulnerable. 'You were upset.'

'Upset! I was bloody mad, but I shouldn't have taken it out on you.' He grinned suddenly. 'We're at it again, aren't we—needling each other and then apologising? And this is only day one. What the devil are we going to do about it, Sister Brown?'

Kate laughed softly. 'Call another truce, I suppose, and resolve to do better tomorrow.'

'But will we, Kate, or will we find something else to have a spat about?'

Her mind flashed back to their conversation in the corridor such a short while ago when he had teased her and touched her cheek so gently.

'You said earlier that we were bound to disagree occasionally but it didn't matter because things would come right in the end,' she said in an expressionless voice.

'Well, I was wrong. I think we need to get things sorted out between us as soon as possible.'

'And how do you propose we do that?'

'By talking—opening up to each other.'

'So, let's talk.'

'Not here—relaxed, over a meal or a drink.' He noted her uncertain expression, and went on, 'A working meal or drink, purely business. I know it's short notice, but could you possibly manage tonight after I've seen Karen's boyfriend?'

For one brief moment she astonished herself by thinking, Could I? Then common sense took over. It would not be a good idea to get involved on a personal level with this charismatic character—it was enough that they had to work together. He'd said purely business, but... You're running scared, whispered a little voice in her head.

'Sorry, not possible.'

'Tomorrow night?'

She shook her head. 'No, I think not. Look, Dr Bruce, I try to keep my work and my leisure time separate.'

'But at our level of commitment to the job work *does* sometimes spill over into leisure time.'

She said indignantly, 'You don't have to tell *me* that. And when it's important of course I work any time of the day or night.'

'Yet you don't consider it important that we spend a

little time trying to achieve a smoother working relationship?' He sounded incredulous.

'Of course it's important, and if you think talking will help then I'm all for it. But why don't we do it over lunch one day? There are plenty of decent restaurants and pubs in or near the town we could get to in a few minutes.'

For a working lunch, she reasoned, sandwiched between the never-ending paperwork and a stint on the wards, would be easier to cope with than an intimate evening meal with its inevitable social overtones. It would all be part of the working day, with no special arrangements to be made at home to cover or explain her absence. And that would be one hell of a bonus, she silently acknowledged.

She glanced across at James, seated at the other side of the desk. 'So, what do you think? Does that meet with your approval, Doctor?'

To her surprise he didn't answer that, but said softly, 'You've a very expressive face, Kate. I wish I knew what was going on in that lovely clever head of yours.'

Kate felt her cheeks reddening. She was angered and flattered at the same time. Anger won. 'Don't patronise me, Dr Bruce,' she said, her voice sharp.

'Sorry, meant it as a compliment,' he said brusquely. 'As to your suggestion for a working lunch, not sure. I've a pretty full diary for the next few days. I'll check it when I get back to my office and let you know when will be convenient. Now. . .' he sat down at the desk '. . .I'll write up Karen's drugs and treatment, and get out of your hair, Sister.'

Well, I made a right mess of that, thought Kate sadly, when he stalked out of the office a little later, having wished her a chilly, 'Good morning and thank you for your help, Sister.' She wanted to reach out and touch his broad, powerful back and beg him not to go.

She felt small, mean and ungrateful. He had offered her an olive branch not once but several times that morning, and she had refused it. And all because she resented—no, stronger than that—feared the fact that she was attracted to him. She hated the thought that for the first time in years a man could ruffle her usual calm, almost throw her off course.

It was a course she had mapped out for herself when she and her husband had finally parted company. There would be no more men in her life, except old and valued friends, at least until the twins had grown up and left home, and probably not even then. She didn't hate men but she was wary of them after her years of being cheated by Paul, who had charmed her into marriage and then abandoned her except when he needed her to bale him out of trouble.

No wonder she was scared of being attracted to another man who exuded charm and charisma. But, of course, James Bruce didn't know this. With all her heart she wished that she hadn't rejected his straightforward, honest attempts to achieve a good working relationship between them. But she had so it would be up to her to put things right, and somehow she would.

As he had said when they'd first met, workwise they were on the same wavelength. And he was right—after working with him for most of the morning she had absolutely no doubts about that. With him, as with her, patients came first. He was a caring doctor. He cared for the whole person and, as Karen White had remarked, he was brilliant.

And 'brilliant' was the adjective Kate found herself using that evening when the twins asked her what the new doctor was like.

'He's brilliant,' she heard herself say, and immediately

wanted to take it back. What a stupid answer to give. What would they make of a remark like that?

Bess gave her a puzzled look across the table. 'What do you mean—brilliant, Mum? I thought you weren't exactly looking forward to having anyone in old Dr Mac's place, yet you sound as if you're pleased as punch about the new doctor.'

'Well, I wasn't looking forward to the change, and I'm still sorry about old Dr Mac having to retire, but I think Dr Bruce will fit in all right. He—he doesn't seem to want to make any sweeping changes, which is what I was most worried about. At least,' she added honestly, remembering the pact they'd made about opening up Theatre for more ops, 'nothing without consulting me first.'

'But brilliant! How d'ya mean—brilliant?' said Philip. 'That's a bit over the top, isn't it, to describe somebody you hardly know? Weird.'

For the only time in her life Kate found herself wishing that her children were not so intelligent and alert or interested in her affairs. In some ways they seemed older than poor young Karen. How could she explain to these bright, perceptive kids of hers that she was impressed by the new man as a doctor, without revealing that James Bruce had made a strong personal impact on her as a man?

By simply saying so, of course, she answered herself. *They* don't know that you haven't been able to get him out of your mind since the day you met him. Neither do they know that you've spent much the of day in a turmoil of mixed emotions on his account. But I've always been so honest with them, her conscience nudged. Then tell them that you like him. There's no harm in that and it's the simple truth.

'Well, maybe brilliant is a bit strong,' she said lightly, making a thing of forking up her salad, 'Though, having seen him at work today, I think it does apply to him as a doctor. He's certainly brilliant at diagnosing and a lot of doctors aren't, and he listens and a lot of doctors don't do that. He was super with the patients.'

She looked up from her plate. Both Bess and Philip were looking at her with bright, enquiring eyes.

Philip said, sounding very grown-up, 'So, the guy's a great doctor, but as a person, Mum, do you like him?'

'That's what I want to know,' said Bess. 'Do you like him as a man?'

Kate thought she detected a hint of anxiety—or possibly belligerence—in her voice.

But that was ridiculous. Why should she be anxious or belligerent? And why had she emphasised *man* when Philip had said *person*? Alarm bells rang as she remembered their conversation the previous week about Bess's friend, Emma Porter, whose mum apparently couldn't live without a man.

Nothing had been said since, but was that what was bothering Bess? Was she still feeling vulnerable in spite of the reassurance Kate had given her then? If so, then the less said about James Bruce the man the better. She back-pedalled on her decision to admit to liking him.

She met their gaze and said firmly, injecting a surprised note into her voice, 'Well, really, I haven't had much time to consider what he's like as a person. Grace and I lunched with him in the canteen but we talked shop most of the time. He was pleasant enough. . .' she shrugged '. . .but I'm not sure that we'll always see eye to eye on how to run things. I guess only time will tell.'

Surely that was innocuous enough and, in fact, was near enough the truth.

Philip's curiosity was obviously satisfied. 'Well, that's OK, then. As long as he doesn't give you too much hassle.' He stood up and pulled a hideous face. 'It's boring, boring problem maths tonight—better go and get on with it. I want to get finished before the wildlife programme.' He paused in the doorway. 'Come on, Bess, we can swap notes.'

'OK, I'll be there,' said Bess grumpily. 'I just want to ask Mum something.'

She turned a serious face to Kate when he had gone. Kate's heart plummeted—now what? 'So, what do you want to ask me, love?'

'Well, what's he like to look at, this Dr Bruce? Is he old, young, fabulously good-looking or what?'

Kate met Bess's unwavering gaze and swallowed an uncomfortable lump in her throat. This was the last thing she had expected—that Bess would be interested in how the new director might look or how old he was when she considered everyone over fourteen ancient.

It was almost like a trick question. She had no option but to be honest over this one. There was no point in prevaricating. At some point Bess would meet up with the doctor and would see for herself that he wasn't exactly ugly.

She said truthfully, 'Well, I'm not sure how old he is—about forty, I should think. As for good-looking, well, I think he is. He's tall, six feet something, has got very thick, dark brown hair and rather nice hazel eyes.' She shrugged. 'And that's it, really. Someday you'll meet him and see for yourself.'

Bess pounced on the one piece of gratuitous information. 'What do you mean—*nice* hazel eyes?'

'Exactly that, though perhaps *kind* would be a better description.' But not when he's angry, she thought, recalling the cold fury in his eyes when he'd fumed about Karen's lack of treatment.

She smiled at Bess, who was frowning, and said firmly,

'Now, love, it's time you stopped grilling me about Dr Bruce. There's nothing more I can tell you about him—I hardly know the man. You get on with your homework and I'll get on with the ironing.'

'But—'

'No buts, Bess. *Finito.*' Her voice was sharp.

'OK, OK,' muttered Bess. 'You don't need come on all heavy, like you were running the hospital.'

'Oh, yes, I do,' said Kate, softening her words with a laugh. 'Sometimes it's absolutely necessary to quell difficult daughters.' She blew Bess a kiss. 'Go on, love, disappear.'

Bess grinned quite suddenly, her smooth rounded cheeks dimpling, and darted round the table to give Kate a bear-like hug. 'You know,' she said fervently, 'as Mums go, you're ace.'

Kate listened to the radio as she did the ironing or, rather she switched it on but made no sense of the jumble of words that were streaming from it as, her mind buzzing, she reviewed the events of the day.

Her first thought was that she finally seemed to have successfully assured Bess that she was not about to do a Mrs Porter and fall for the first eligible man to replace an ex-husband. That was an enormous relief. But would it be possible to disguise the fact indefinitely from her and Philip that she found James Bruce attractive, as a person as well as a doctor?

Not very likely, she thought uneasily. The three of them were used to discussing the day's happenings over supper. It was a habit she'd encouraged since they were very small to make up for their father's absence. 'You tell me about your day,' she would say, 'and I'll tell you all about mine.'

It was a way of reassuring them when she had to leave

them with her parents or at nursery school, while she went out to work, so that they knew exactly where she was and what she was doing. And she did the same when she went out occasionally to meet up with friends, both male and female. And it worked. They knew about her friends and she knew about theirs.

Not, she reminded herself, wryly, that she had any desire to reveal the fact that James Bruce had an extraordinary effect on her, and that she was aware of some peculiar vibes flowing between them. No way. That was something that would remain her secret. All she wanted to do was admit to her children that she liked the man, and perhaps in time would number him amongst her friends.

If only Emma Porter's mum hadn't thrown a spanner in the works it would have been easy to explain that she found him attractive, both as a man and a doctor, and she was looking forward to working with him. Bess and Philip would have been pleased for her and—

The telephone rang, and by the time she'd had a lively conversation with her mother it was time to pack up the unfinished ironing and sit down and be soothed by David Attenborough, working his magic with the animals.

After the wildlife programme came the news. Then there was a last-minute sorting out of lunch money and sports gear for the next day before the twins finally took themselves off to bed.

She suddenly felt exhausted. She was too tired to bath, but had a quick shower and fell into bed. Too many things had happened today, she mused hazily, switching off the bedside lamp and snuggling down under the duvet. No wonder I'm whacked. A moment later she slipped into oblivion and slept soundly till morning.

* * *

It was a blue and gold jewel of a morning.

As Kate neared the top of the drive on her way to work James drove slowly past in his car. He would have stopped but she waved him on, making it clear that she wanted to walk. He nodded, lifted his hand in salute and accelerated away from her.

He was standing by his parked car as she rounded the last bend, obviously waiting for her. The sun glinted on his dark brown glossy hair which ruffled in the light breeze coming off the sea. The stern lines of his face, lit by the clear early morning sunshine, looked chiselled, refined, and his jaw square and thrusting, his shoulders broad and powerful.

She had sensed that he would be there, yet her heart thudded painfully as, in a dream, she drifted across the gravelled concourse toward him. It was an unreal sensation.

With long, easy strides he strode to meet her, but stopped a few yards away from her.

'Why didn't you tell me, Kate?' he asked mildly. 'I would have understood.'

Kate stopped drifting and dropped to earth with a bump. She wasn't sure what she had expected, but it wasn't this. She swiftly composed herself, swallowing surprise, dismay and embarrassment. Remembering how formally they had parted the previous day, she asked politely, 'Tell you what, Dr Bruce?'

'The real reason why you don't want to meet me for an evening meal.'

Her vulnerable heart played another trick on her and seemed to stand still. She felt blood rush to her cheeks and then recede. However perceptive he was, how could he have guessed that she was scared stiff of allowing herself to get too friendly with him? Too scared because she was so deeply attracted to him. That was her secret.

She scrabbled around in her mind to find something to explain her feelings, make light of them, but before she could utter a word he said, with the faintest of smiles, 'If only you'd explained that you've got children to care for I'd have understood. It must be tough being a single mum and holding down a responsible job. No wonder you're so protective of your leisure time.'

Kate felt winded as a tide of relief flooded through her. He hadn't guessed. Somehow she found her voice, though it came out a bit shaky and breathless.

'I didn't realise that you didn't know—everybody does, you see. The twins come up to help amuse the little ones in the play group occasionally. They know all the staff and the other children who come during the school holidays—it's rather like a holiday camp then,' she said, with a rather forced little laugh.

Then she added, in case he should think that the child-minding facilities might encroach on the hospital, 'A very well-organised camp, with trained helpers.'

James gave a restrained bellow of laughter, and said gently, 'Oh, Kate, you're still on the defensive with me, aren't you? I'm in favour of the play centre, remember? And of course it's well organised if you had anything to do with it.'

He looked round the car park, deserted except for a few cars belonging to night staff, and took a step forward to close the gap between them. He reached out and took both his hands on his.

'Let's make a bargain, Kate, to be honest with each other from now on—and what could be better than sealing it with a kiss?' he said, and, bending down, kissed her firmly on the mouth.

She stood rooted to the spot, staring up at him, until he

took her arm and—talking what might have been a load of gobbledegook for all the sense she could make of it—he steered her through the main entrance and down the corridor to her office.

How long she would have sat and stared into space, trying to make sense out of what had just happened between her and James, if the phone hadn't trilled into life she had no idea, but the world suddenly slotted into perspective as the working day proper began with a string of staff problems to be solved.

The call that jerked Kate out of her reverie and into action was from Dora Cross, reporting that she was an assistant nurse short and as it was ops day she needed a replacement.

'I know it's early,' she apologised, 'but the list starts at eight so I need cover stat.'

'I'll get someone lined up,' promised Kate.

A few minutes later Colin Peel, the registered charge nurse paramedic who as unit manager ran the minor injuries unit with amazing efficiency, rang in to say that he seemed to have picked up some sort of tummy bug and was feeling pretty rotten at that moment.

'But I'll try to make it later,' he said, 'when I stop throwing up.'

'No way,' said Kate firmly. 'We can do without your bugs, thanks very much. Do the usual, Colin. Keep warm, take plenty of fluids. You know the drill. See your GP if you're no better tomorrow and go officially sick. By the way, who's providing medical cover on MIU today?'

'Well, this morning Doc Wilson, and this afternoon none other than our new man, Dr Bruce. He offered to relieve Doc Wilson, who was moaning about missing a golf tournament. Madge Beamish is senior staff today and can act up. She's OK, though occasionally gets a bit rattled. I'm sorry to let you down, Kate. Be back as soon as poss.'

So James was stepping into the breach just as he'd promised he would—the laparoscopy on Stephanie Pye this morning, the MIU this afternoon.

She reassured her conscientious charge nurse, 'Don't worry, Colin, I'll keep an eye on things.'

The phone rang again as soon as she replaced the receiver. It was Madge Beamish.

'I'm so sorry, Sister, but I won't be in today. My mother had a mild coronary last night and was admitted to the General in Porthampton. I want to stay with her but, depending on how things go, I'll try to get in tomorrow. Will you let Colin know, please?'

'Of course. Don't worry about a thing, Madge,' Kate agreed mendaciously, having no intention of telling her that Colin was off sick. 'You just be there for your mother, and let me know if there is anything I can do. Don't hurry back—we'll manage.'

Setting all personal problems ruthlessly aside, she recradled the receiver, rested her chin on her hands and reviewed the situation.

The afternoon would be tricky, with no regular senior staff on duty and a doctor who, however brilliant, was unfamiliar with the routine. James Bruce would handle whatever turned up in the way of injuries with consummate skill but he would need guiding through the internal procedures peculiar to the Memorial—the discharge, aftercare or the occasional transfer of a patient to a larger hospital for specialised treatment.

Colin would have been the perfect guide and mentor—not pushy but quietly supportive, unerringly steering the new man through the maze of paperwork that bugged modern medicine, was hated by the doctors and loved by the back-room boys.

Well, there was no Colin and no Madge. But on the plus side there was Pat Kenyon, the bright junior staff nurse, and two eminently sensible, MIU-trained nursing assistants who could be relied upon utterly. And Madge could be covered by calling in one of the senior staff nurses on standby who had experience on the minor injuries unit.

Covering the skillful, experienced Colin was the problem. The solution was staring her in the face. With her knowledge of the department and procedures, she would have to stand in for Colin and take over as temporary unit manager.

A prickle of pleasure shafted through her. OK, there might be some awkwardness between her and James on account of the kiss, but she looked forward to working with him. Surely, if he'd meant what he'd said earlier he would be equally pleased to work with her and make yet another fresh start, and this time make it work.

Well, she would play her part. This afternoon she wouldn't give him the chance to needle her into a confrontation—she would handle him with kid gloves.

CHAPTER FIVE

KATE only saw James once during the morning when she was doing her general round, and then not to speak to. He was deep in conversation with Stephanie Pye who had just arrived back from Theatre, having had her laparoscopy. Obviously he was talking to her about the results of the internal examination and Kate, not wanting to interrupt, walked quietly past the bed.

Her pulse, though, quickened at the sight of him and she had to make a tremendous effort not to dwell on how superb he looked in theatre greens as she continued with her rounds. But long practice at squashing personal intrusive thoughts enabled her to dismiss his image and carry on as usual, ensuring that all was well with patients and staff as she visited each department.

In Colin's absence, she visited the minor injuries unit several times and found it blessedly quiet, with never more than one or two patients waiting to be seen and sometimes no one at all. In fact, on one occasion when she popped in she found John Wilson swinging a club in the doctors' office and Ellie Ford, the relief senior staff nurse, and Pat Kenyon, her junior, helping the care nurses tidy cubicles and cupboards.

'All quiet on the western front,' said Ellie cheerfully. 'I wonder if it's the lull before the storm?'

Prophetic words, thought Kate as the waiting area began to fill up soon after she arrived to head the nursing team at one o'clock.

On her arrival she had sent Ellie off for her lunch break, but Pat and the two assistants had already had their breaks and were able to deal with the sudden influx of patients, taking names and brief histories of their injuries.

Dr Wilson and Bruce were still closeted in the office, doing the official change-over.

As Ellie had explained gleefully, before zooming off to lunch, 'Doc Wilson's champing at the bit, dying to get off to the golf course. He was halfway out of the door the moment Dr Bruce arrived, but our fabulously dishy new doctor insisted on having all the gen before he disappeared.'

'And quite right, too,' Kate replied with a chuckle, her heart beat soaring at Ellie's flattering description of James.

It was another ten minutes before John Wilson emerged from the doctors' office. He lifted his hand to Kate in passing, and muttered, 'Well, I'm off at last—it's all yours, Kate.' He added, with a jerk of his head toward the office as he made his way to the staff exit, 'Good luck with the new boy—you'll need it.'

Kate was at the blackboard, chalking up the names of patients she had earlier assessed in order of priority.

She laughed. 'Thanks for the warning, John. Good luck with the tournament.' She turned back to the board which was attached to the wall just outside the office and added the last name to the list.

A moment later James Bruce appeared in the doorway, filling it with his breadth and height. Had he heard her exchange with John Wilson? He was smiling broadly, his eyes brimming with amusement. Of course he had, she realised ruefully. He'd heard every word and was enjoying her discomfort at being discovered. Yet even as colour flooded her face she found herself smiling back at him.

What was it with this man that he could make her smile so readily?

James was fascinated by the rosy glow that spread over her high, rounded cheek-bones, making dark pools of her violet-blue eyes. What a stunning woman, he thought as she turned back to the board and her bronzed chestnut bob of hair swung like a silk curtain against her blushing cheeks. Difficult to imagine her being the mother of eleven-year-old twins—incredible. He couldn't believe that he'd had the nerve to kiss her. If only, he wished...

He crushed the wish and moved away from the door to stand beside her and study the board.

Kate tried not to notice his nearness, tried to forget the disturbing kiss he'd bestowed on her that morning. He had removed his tweedy jacket and rolled up his sleeves ready for action, but he still smelt tangy and tweedy. It struck her that in an old war film he would have been the tall, dark, chunky, pipe-smoking hero. What an odd idea to have, she thought in astonishment.

The dark curly hairs on his bare arm brushed against her own arm, sending shock waves crackling up to the back of her neck.

She moved away from him fractionally putting an inch or so between them, and immediately wished she hadn't. Perhaps he hadn't noticed.

'Sorry,' he murmured, and moved a little the other way, putting more inches between them as he continued to stare at the board. 'I see you've assessed them—good. So, what have we got here?' He pointed to the first name.

God, she must get hold of herself. She took a deep breath and reeled off the details. 'Six-year-old girl, Naomi Spence, fell over. Forearm grossly swollen, some tenderness over area. Thought it might be a simple or greenstick fracture so I've put it in a sling pro tem. Child very stoic, but Mrs Spence is pretty rattled.'

'Right, sounds like an X-ray job. Let's go and have a look-see. Lead on, Sister.'

He followed her into the number one cubicle and she introduced him to the mother and child. He made some reassuring remarks to Mrs Spence as Kate removed the sling from the girl's arm then, bending over the couch, he gently supported the small distorted limb as he inspected it.

'Does it hurt much, love?' he asked.

A frown appeared above the sloe-black eyes. 'Well, a bit,' she replied, 'when I move it.'

'That's why your arm was put into a sling—to keep it still. I think you may have broken this bone just here, Naomi.' He pointed a spot midway between her elbow and wrist. 'But to make sure we're going to take a picture of it.' He turned to her mother, hovering by anxiously. 'Sister will arrange for someone to go with you to the X-ray department, Mrs Spence, and I'll see you again later.'

James waited as Kate replaced the sling and assured Mrs Spence that someone would come for her shortly.

They left the cubicle together and walked toward the main office area, where the general paperwork was done and various forms and files were kept in pigeon-holes above the long wall desk.

'You were right.' He perched himself on the edge of a stool and began to fill in the X-ray form that Kate placed in front of him. 'That child's almost certainly got a fractured radius, but hopefully a simple greenstick that'll only need immobilising. What's the drill if it's confirmed, and it needs a plaster job done on it? Do you have someone on call for that?'

'I can do it and so can Ellie—Ellie Ford, the senior staff

nurse. She's on lunch break at the moment, but will be back soon.'

'Right, that's good.' He raised his head and gave her a long, searching look as he handed her the completed form. Their fingers touched, trembled, recoiled. He said gruffly, 'What the hell. . .?' But he didn't finish the sentence. They continued to stare at each other for mind-stretching moments in taut silence.

Then Kate tore her eyes away from his, waved the form and muttered breathlessly, 'I'll get this sorted out.'

'Before you do,' said James, his voice sounding so normal that Kate, practically hyperventilating, wondered if she had imagined the extraordinary mind-blowing exchange that had just taken place, 'fill me in on the lad in cubicle two.'

Fierce anger and sheer professionalism came to her aid. If he wanted to pretend that nothing had happened it was OK by her. Perhaps he wanted to pretend that this morning's kiss hadn't happened either. Well, that was OK, too. In fact, it was fine. It shouldn't have happened and she wished with all her heart that it hadn't. She had been temporarily overwhelmed by his charisma, that was all.

No way could she know that he, too, had been totally overwhelmed by what had happened, had been shocked to the core to find himself reacting to her like a schoolboy and was playing for time as he came to terms with it.

In an icy cool voice she rattled out details. 'Trevor Cade, sixteen, amateur hurdler, practising over the groynes on the beach, gashed and grazed shin, some splinters of wood in wound. Feeling sorry for himself and a bit silly.'

'Thank you. I'll take a look at him right now.' Still neither his voice nor eyes gave anything away. Apparently her coolness didn't bother him one bit.

'I'll get things organised for the little Spence girl to go

for her X-ray.' Kate's voice was as colourless as she could make it.

Kate saw Naomi and her mother off to the X-ray department in the care of Irene, one of the assistant nurses, and arrived in cubicle two just as James had finished his examination of the injured hurdler and was explaining to Trevor what was going to happen.

'First this area round the wound will be numbed with a local anaesthetic, then Sister will remove the splinters, clean it up with antiseptic, stitch the cut together and cover it with a protective dressing.' He gave the young lad one of his reassuring smiles, then glanced across at Kate with an incredibly gentle expression in his warm hazel eyes and enquired, 'Is that all right with you, Sister?'

The smouldering warmth in his eyes made her catch and hold her breath. Why was he looking at her like that when minutes before he had been totally indifferent? Bereft of words as this sudden metamorphosis, she could only nod her agreement.

'Good.' His voice was low, husky, full of the most astonishingly tender overtones. 'Then I'll leave you to it, Sister. Our ambitious young hurdler's all yours.' Swishing aside the curtain, he left the cubicle.

Kate stared after him in stunned silence. What was all that about—not what he'd said but the way that he'd said it?

Trevor cleared his throat nervously, making her jump.

She gathered herself together, smiled at him and, smoothly shifting into nurse mode, set about putting him at his ease as she assembled the instruments and dressings she would need to treat him. He was obviously regretting his silly attempt to jump the groynes, and was scared stiff about the state of his leg.

Talking quietly all the time, she methodically picked

out the shards of wood from the extensively grazed shin, which—in spite of the anaesthetic—was a painful process. It was some twenty minutes before the job was completed and she was able to send him on his way, if not rejoicing, certainly much relieved. She provided him with a couple of pain-killing tablets to be taken when the effects of the injection wore off.

'And come back in five days' time to have the stitches removed, Trevor,' she reminded him as he limped away with an embarrassed mumble of thanks.

The busy afternoon flashed past as a continuous stream of people arrived, sporting a variety of cuts, bruises, sprains, headaches and tummy aches—the usual beginning to the start of the summer season.

Kate was glad to be rushed off her feet as she constantly renewed her efforts to relegate James and his singular behaviour to the back of her mind. It wasn't easy as they frequently came in contact with each other, but she avoided him when she could. When possible, she sent Ellie or Pat to assist him.

She took on more than her fair share of patients, skilfully chatting to them and reassuring them as she dressed their wounds with her practical, competent hands. She immersed herself in work, and at James's direction performed the support plaster bandaging job on little Naomi when the X-rays confirmed a greenstick fracture.

The staff she directed in her usual pleasant, decisive manner so that the department ran like clockwork. The dressing trolleys were kept stocked up, cubicles kept tidy and everyone was promptly and sympathetically greeted as they came through the door.

Somehow she kept her turbulent thoughts at bay, playing the part of the efficient, much-admired sister in charge so successfully that none of her colleagues guessed at what was going on beneath her placid exterior.

But James knew. He wasn't deceived for an instant because he was doing much the same thing, keeping up a façade. To the staff and patients he was an unfailingly kind, calm, caring doctor, unfazed by any situation, but beneath the calm raged several conflicting emotions. Taking a few minutes' breather in the office, he took stock of his feelings.

He was puzzled, happy, amazed and a little anxious. He knew that something special was happening to him and, he thought—dared to hope—to Kate. And something marvellous *had* happened when their hands had touched. It had shaken him to the core, and he had let it show. He hadn't been able to hide it when they worked together— she must have seen it in his eyes whenever he looked at her, heard it in his voice whenever he spoke to her.

Perhaps he should have been more discreet but, what the hell, he didn't want to be discreet and saw no reason why he should be. He was a free agent and Kate a grown woman, with very much a mind of her own, so there was no reason why...if she wanted to... His spirits soared— then plummeted. In his euphoria he'd forgotten the children.

How the hell had he forgotten them? He was a free agent, but she wasn't. Her children were her life—'I like to keep my leisure time free,' she'd said, and only later had he discovered why. So, did he stand a chance? However she felt about him, would she...?

There was a tap at the half-open office door and Shirley, one of the assistant nurses, popped her head round and said briskly, 'Doctor, Sister Brown says will you come, please. We've got what might be a bleeder in cubical five.'

James was on his feet and out of the office as she

finished speaking. Kate wanted him—a patient needed him. 'Do you mean a haemophiliac?' he asked, striding toward the cubicles.

'Sister's not sure. The man walked in and fainted before we could get anything out of him, but he's bleeding like a stuck—sorry—profusely from the rectum.'

They reached the cubicle.

The 'bleeder', a man somewhere in his mid-twenties, naked from the waist downwards, was lying almost prone on his left side on the examination bed which had been raised at the foot to its maximum.

There seemed to be a lot of blood about but, then, a little blood went a long way. It was on the man's bare legs and buttocks, and on Kate's plastic apron. With the heel of her hand she was pressing a thick wedge of cloth between the buttocks into the rectum, but dark, sticky blood was oozing through and round it.

She glanced up at James, who was already standing beside her. 'False alarm, I think. It's beginning to ease off, but it needs more pressure,' she said breathlessly. 'Can't be sure, but I think it's coming from external haemorrhoids.' She lifted the pad slightly and James bent and peered at the bloody mess beneath.

'Probably,' he grunted, as she clamped the pad back into position. 'I'll take over for a moment—heavier-handed than you are.' He gave her a quick, slanting smile. 'Let's have another clean pad, please, Nurse.'

He held out a hand to Pat Kenyon, who was standing the other side of the couch. She tore off another chunk of cloth and slapped it firmly onto his outstretched palm, as if passing an instrument to the surgeon in Theatre.

'Thanks.' He nodded to Kate. 'Ready?' His plastic-gloved hand hovered an inch above hers.

'Ready.'

Smoothly they changed positions so that the pressure on the patient's rectum was uninterrupted.

The man's eyelids flickered.

'He's coming to,' said Pat.

'Good.' James nodded at the staff nurse. 'As soon as he's round we'll get some info from him. Meanwhile, Sister, will you check on his pulse and blood pressure, please? Might have to push in some fluids or even blood if it's too low. 'Can't tell with haemorrhoids.'

The sphygmomanometer was on the dressings trolley at Pat's side of the high bed, and Kate stayed round that side to take her readings, fixing the cuff of the sphygmo round the patient's free right arm.

He recovered full alertness as she was inflating the cuff.

His name, he said in a quavery voice, was Ian Thompson. He was twenty-six, and suffered from piles which he was waiting to have operated on. He lived in London, but was presently visiting his parents in Millchester. He had suddenly been conscious of something warm running down his legs and had felt strange as he was passing the hospital drive so had naturally turned in.

He wasn't a haemophiliac, but he'd had some bleeding from his piles over the last few weeks. 'But nothing like this,' he said, catching sight of his stained legs.

'It's all right,' said Kate soothingly, and echoing James's thought. 'A little blood goes a long way. We'll get you cleaned up as soon as the bleeding's stopped.' She finished taking his blood pressure, deflated the cuff and looked across at James. 'Pulse steady, a hundred. BP's a bit low at eighty over sixty.'

James's eyes gleamed. 'Not bad, not bad at all, considering the initial blood loss,' he murmured in a low, satisfied voice, as if she had said something remarkable. He glanced round at the three nurses, his glance lingering for a moment on Kate. 'Jolly good, everyone. Nice bit of prompt first-aiding. Blood pressure might have fallen considerably lower without it—good teamwork.'

Pat and Shirley looked pleased and surprised in equal measure. This sort of unstinted praise didn't often come their way. He really was brilliant to work with.

Kate thought so, too, but said rather stiffly, 'Just doing our job.'

'Is everything all right?' asked Ian.

'You're doing fine,' assured James. 'Your blood pressure's a bit low, but should start to improve. We'll take it again in a minute. Now, let's see what's going on here.' He lifted the pad and inspected it. There was very little blood on it. He bent down and carefully examined the rectal area. 'Good, bleeding's virtually stopped—seems to be clotting nicely.'

He straightened up and looked across the bed at Pat. 'Now, Staff, will you please prepare a zinc oxide dressing and fix it in place.' He patted the patient's shoulder. 'This dressing will help reduce the pain and itching and the chance of further bleeding,' he explained.

'Thanks, Doctor, that'll be a relief. Will I be able to go then?'

'Yes, in about half an hour, after we've taken your blood pressure again and slowly get you horizontal and then into a sitting position. And I want you to start drinking. You need plenty of fluids to make up for some you've lost—don't want you getting dehydrated. How are you going to get home? You certainly won't be fit to walk or to on the bus. I'm going to give you an additional painkiller by injection and it might make you a bit woozy.'

'My father will pick me up if someone would phone him for me and explain what's happened.'

'No problem,' said Kate. 'Shirley can do that for you presently.'

'There, all fixed up.' James looked immensely pleased, as if she'd performed another minor miracle, and added, 'And now, Sister, if you would kindly draw up thirty milligrams of codeine phosphate I'll give Ian his jab.'

Would she kindly draw up? Of course she would—it was her job. Puzzled but obedient, Kate collected the codeine phosphate from the locked drug cupboard, filled the syringe and handed it to James. *I could have done this and saved him the time,* she thought as she watched him swab Ian's arm and slide the needle smoothly into the firm muscle, *but he seems to want to do it. It's as if. . .*

James dropped the used syringe into the receiver and handed it back to her with a murmur of thanks.

He looked down at the patient. 'There we are, Ian, all done. I'll leave the nurses to make you comfortable. And when you return to London go and see your GP. I'll give you a letter to take back, explaining about this haemorrhage—might speed up your hospital treatment. Call for it at Reception on your way out.'

'You're very kind, Doctor. In fact, you've all been marvellous. Thank you.' Ian smiled pallidly round at everyone. 'I don't know how you do mucky jobs like this.' He shuddered. 'I certainly couldn't.'

'Each to his own,' said James. 'Good luck to you, Mr Thompson. The sooner you get those piles fixed the better.' He stripped off his gloves, threw them into the bin and turned to Kate. 'When you can spare a moment, Sister, a word, please.'

His words said *at your convenience,* but his eyes aid *now, immediately, pronto,* and he underlined it by holding the cubicle curtain to one side and waiting for her.

What could he want to see her about? Not the work—

that had gone without a hitch. In fact, he'd piled on the praise. Kate's heart thudded. She felt elated, yet knew that she shouldn't. It was all wrong.

She said with amazing calm, 'I might as well come right now. I'm sure Pat and Shirley can manage for a bit.'

Pat and Shirley murmured that they could, and exchanged significant looks. It was as plain as a pikestaff that something was going on between the doctor and Sister, but what? Another morsel for the grapevine?

Kate discarded her bloody apron and gloves and slipped past James and out of the cubicle.

He took her arm. It tingled where his fingers rested and she stiffened. 'This way, Kate,' he said softly, steering her past the other cubicles toward the doctors' office. 'We need to talk.'

Play it cool, play it innocent. 'We've agreed to do that one lunchtime, to iron out our working relationship, though I thought this afternoon—'

'Kate, you know damn well I don't mean that,' he interrupted as he edged her through the door into the office and pushed it shut with his foot. 'I mean about us.' He put his hands on her shoulders and turned her round to face him.

It was important not to look at him. She stared fixedly at his jazzy tie.

Her voice shook as she said quietly, 'Us! There is no us, James. We hardly know each other. Work is all we have in common.'

'Oh, come on, Kate, you know that's not true. We've been walking a tightrope all afternoon. I've been making an absolute fool of myself, almost maudlin. Please look at me.' He put his fingers under her chin and tilted her face upwards.

She closed her eyes.

'You've got to look at me sometime.' His voice was gentle, yet urgent. 'You can't go around with your eyes closed all the time, either physically or emotionally. Something's happened between us, and we've got to acknowledge it. It started the day we met. Pretending it didn't isn't going to make it go away.'

He was right. Kate opened her eyes and stared straight into his. There was no laughter in them. they were all muted greens and browns—serious, thoughtful. What could he see in hers? She tried to blank out any expression—mustn't give herself away. Who're you kidding? scoffed an inner voice. You already have.

'Good, that's a start,' he said. 'Now, when are we going to meet properly, I mean one evening, to talk this through?'

She took a deep breath. She mustn't give in, mustn't. 'I've already explained—'

'I know,' he broke in. 'You try to keep your evenings free for your children. Very commendable, quite right, understood, but don't tell me that you never go out. You must have some social life of your own. Grace mentioned—'

'Grace!' she exploded, taking a step back from him. 'How dare you discuss me with Grace?'

She went hot and cold. Had Grace told him about Paul and his charisma and the mess they had made of their marriage? Grace in whom, in a rare moment of misery, she had once confided that she had felt diminished as a woman—guilty for not making her marriage work. Would she tell *him* of all people—this near-stranger who had walked into her life a week ago, spreading his own charisma and shaking her to the core?

Anguished, angry, frightened by the depth of the feelings he aroused in her, she stared at the solid, rock-like man who faced her.

His dark, thick eyebrows were pulled together in a fierce frown over his bony nose. 'We were doing no such thing, Kate. We weren't discussing you. We were talking theatre—not operating, drama. She said you and she were both members of the local theatre club and could introduce me if I wanted to become a member. It follows that you occasionally go out in the evenings, and so you could free up an evening to go out with me.'

Kate wished that the floor would open and swallow her up. Grace was her friend and the soul of discretion. Of course she hadn't said anything. And James—James wouldn't probe behind her back. He was too straightforward for that—she had learned that when she had practically accused him of spying on her staff.

Yet here she was, doubting him again. What on earth had got into her? Why did she do it—keep finding fault with him, creating difficulties? The answer came clear and loud. Because she had to. If she didn't she would let him into her life and she mustn't do that because of the children—they were all that mattered. She must protect them. She had no right to allow herself to be attracted to this man. Attracted! Who was she kidding? It didn't even begin to describe her feelings towards him.

Quite suddenly, to her horror, she felt her eyes swimming with tears. She said shakily, 'I. . .I'm so sorry, James. Stupid thing to say, to accuse. . .' To her further horror, the tears spilled over and trickled down her cheeks and she couldn't stop them.

It was like a knife to his heart, seeing her cry. He took one stride toward her, opened his arms wide and folded her to him.

She—practical Kate, who seldom cried—laid her head on his broad chest and let the tears flow, soaking his shirt and tie. She could hear his heart thudding rhythmically, loudly, 'Sorry,' she mumbled. 'Sorry.'

He stroked her bob of shining hair. 'It's been a difficult day, Kate. Have a good howl, do you good. Wish I could join you.' And very gently he dropped a kiss on the top of her head.

She lifted her head and blinked up at him through tear-drenched violet blue eyes. 'Has it been difficult for you, too?' she asked. He'd been so cool, at times almost indifferent.

He gave a short bark of laughter. 'You could say that,' he said dryly.

Kate sniffed and silently James produced a large white handkerchief. 'I've got a tissue here,' she said, fumbling in her uniform pocket.

'Useless,' he said. 'Take this and have a good blow.' He pushed his handkerchief into her hand.

She took it, slipped out of the haven of his arms, blew her nose hard and gave him a watery smile.

His eyes brightened and his mouth twitched at the corners. She looked like a vulnerable little girl. 'Better?' he asked.

'Yes, thanks.' She stuffed the hanky into her pocket. 'I'll return it to you after I've washed it.'

He was brusque. 'Whenever, it doesn't matter. What does matter is what we're going to do about us. We've got to meet, Kate, and the sooner the better—get ourselves sorted out. You name the day and time and I'll fit in.'

There was no more fight left in her, and she wasn't even sure that she wanted to fight any more. For some reason, the idea of telling Bess and Philip that she was going out for a meal with her new boss suddenly seemed less daunting. They would, she was sure, understand that it was a professional courtesy as one senior to another. Liar, said her inner voice. Just a little white lie, she pleaded, until—

'Friday evening,' she said briskly. 'The children are staying over with friends for the night. Shall we say seven-thirty at Harbour Lights—that's the pub near the lighthouse about a mile west of here. We could meet there but go on somewhere else, if you want to.'

'Friday seems a hell of a long way off.'

'Only three days. Sorry, it's the best I can do.'

He shrugged and gave her a lopsided smile. 'So be it. But is there any reason why I shouldn't pick you up from the lodge?'

'Staff, visitors, the grapevine will be buzzing if you're seen collecting me.'

'Does it matter? We have nothing to hide, and you presumably intend telling your children that we're having a meal together.'

'Of course.'

'Then, if they know, there's no earthly reason why I shouldn't collect you from the lodge, is there, Kate?' Questioningly, his eyes held hers.

'No,' she murmured, feeling wave after wave of warmth and understanding rippling out from him, 'no reason at all.'

'Then trust me,' he said softly.

All doubt had fled. She had never felt so sure of anything in her life. 'Oh, I do,' she whispered. 'I do, I trust you with—Oh!' She stopped abruptly as there was a rap at the door.

'Sounds like duty, knocking at the door,' said James. They pulled funny, sympathetic faces at each other, then he turned and opened the door.

'Afraid it's me again, Doctor, Sister,' said Shirley apologetically, glancing at them both. 'A couple of boys collided on their bikes and they're a bit battered. Will you come and check them over?'

'We're on our way,' said James, and led the way to the cubicles.

By five o'clock the volume of people turning up for treatment had slowed to a trickle, and Kate sent Shirley and Irene off duty. There was no need for them to stay on till the unit closed at seven.

It was suddenly very quiet except for a murmur of voices from behind cubicle curtains, where Ellie was assisting James who was stitching up a badly gashed hand and Pat was dealing with a case of sunburn.

Kate looked round the empty waiting room and tidied up a few magazines. There was nothing else to do so she thought she would pop along to her own office and attend to any messages. But she would return later to see that was all was well, before locking up for the night, and, she thought with a frisson of pleasure, say goodnight to James.

She peeped round the curtain of number three cubicle. His head bent, James was intent on his stitching, but both the patient and Ellie looked up as the curtain swooshed open.

Kate smiled at the patient, apologised to him and to the top of James's head for butting in and said to Ellie, 'Nothing doing out here so I'm going back to my office. That's where I'll be if you want me. I've sent Shirley and Irene off, but Pat's nearly finished and will soon be free to circulate.'

'Instead of going back to your wretched office, why don't you get off early for once? The twins will be glad to see you,' said Ellie cheerfully. 'We can cope here till seven.'

Without looking up, James said with equal cheerfulness, 'What a good idea. Go on, Sister, scoot. Like Staff says, it'll be nice for you to be able to spend some extra time with your kids.'

'Well, if you're sure. . .' He needn't sound so cheerful, she thought peevishly, as if he would be glad to see me gone.

'Positive,' said James, tying off the last stitch. 'There we are, Mr Taylor. Nurse will put a dressing on that and tell you when to come back to have the stitches out.' He straightened and grinned at Kate as he peeled off his gloves. 'You still here, Sister?' His eyes teased gently. 'Go home, have a nice evening and don't worry about a thing—I'll lock up, trust me.'

'Oh, I do,' said Kate for the second time that afternoon. 'I'll be off, then. Goodnight—see you tomorrow, Ellie, and you, Dr Bruce.' And, with nod, she whisked herself out of the cubicle.

CHAPTER SIX

ON CLOUD nine, as she floated down the drive, Kate savoured the teasing gentle expression which had lit James's eyes as he'd shooed her off duty. Her euphoria persisted, though she had yet to decide how to tell Bess and Philip that he had invited her out for a meal on Friday.

And she still hadn't found the answer by the time she arrived at the lodge. Oh, well, she thought on a wave of optimism, buoyed up by her happiness, it's in the lap of the gods. I'll just have to trust to luck that I find the right words.

Luck was on her side and, in the event, it turned out to be remarkably easy to find the right words for over supper they asked her what she was going to do with herself while they were staying overnight with their friend, Craig Wallace.

Was she going out with Grace, or going over to see Granny and Grandpa? they wanted to know.

Kate glowed, touched as always by their genuine interest and concern. They really were the most loving kids.

She chose her words with care and kept it simple. 'Well, as a matter of fact, she said, 'our new medical director, Dr Bruce, has asked me out to dinner—you know, as one colleague to another. There's such a lot to discuss, and we're both so busy that we never seem the have time when we're on duty.'

'Oh, you mean a sort of working dinner,' said Philip, surprising her, as he often did, by his grasp of the adult world, 'like business executives—they're always having working breakfasts and lunches and things, planning future strategy and all that stuff.'

'Yes, that about sums it up,' said Kate, subduing a guilty blush and inwardly heaving a sigh of relief. With Philip's innocent help, she had got her small—or *not* so small, nagged an inner voice—deception across without difficulty.

Surely, even Bess would be quite reassured and satisfied by this explanation.

A trifle nervously, she glanced across at her daughter.

Bess pulled a face. 'Sounds utterly, utterly boring,' she said, tossing her head so that her long plait rested on her shoulder. Casually, with a throwaway gesture, she flipped it back so that it hung down her spine.

It was a new mannerism, a growing-up mannerism—almost coquettish, noted Kate affectionately, just as 'utterly' was apparently the new in word. Her spirits soared. Clearly, Bess was quite unimpressed by her news and totally reassured, and that at the moment was all that mattered. Presenting her date with James as business, rather than purely pleasure, had been justified.

She felt she could be a little more expansive, and said brightly, 'Oh, I don't think it will be boring at all, love. We'll be talking medicine, exchanging ideas about treatment and the general running of the hospital. We'll both enjoy that—'

Bess interrupted, 'Oh, medicine talk—that's not boring, it's fab. I thought you meant business business—money and things.'

'No fear, James—Dr Bruce—doesn't like admin stuff any more than I do. He wants to leave that to Grace and her staff when possible, though it's inevitable that he'll get somewhat involved, just as I am. He's all for pursuing policies to benefit the patients, and he seems to have lots of good ideas.'

'Your Dr Bruce sounds utterly brilliant,' said Bess, rolling her eyes dramatically. 'Quite fab.'

Old-fashioned 'fab', apparently, had made a comeback and was yet another current in word.

'Yeah, he seems an OK sort of guy,' said Philip.

They both approved of him. Kate went pink with pleasure.

He's a very, very OK sort of guy, she wanted to enthuse, but instead said mildly, 'Yes, I think he's a very nice man, and we certainly see eye to eye where patient care is concerned.' Then, metaphorically crossing her fingers and hoping that she wasn't pushing her luck, she added, 'It'll be quite interesting to get to know something about him personally, too. I'm really looking forward to Friday evening.'

She waited for their reaction. The heavens didn't fall in. Bess didn't burst into tears.

'Good. Hope you have a great time, Mum,' they said in unison, and then went on to burble gaily, like any other children, about their own plans for Friday evening.

To celebrate Craig's twelfth birthday, they told her gleefully, there was to be a barbecue and a disco on the roomy patio of the spacious Wallace residence, overlooking the estuary. And, of course, they would swim in the simply fabulous new swimming pool that had recently been built and was floodlit at night.

In a daze of relief Kate listened and occasionally joined in their happy chatter. Relief that she had told them that she was going out with James and had even admitted to liking him, and they hadn't minded. It was a beginning, and she had been as frank as she dared. She could hardly have said more. There was nothing else could she have told them.

Nothing! There was a limit to frankness, she decided, and she had reached it. No way could she explain to her eleven-year-old offspring, however bright and mature they were, that she was wildly, deeply drawn to a man she had only just met. It was unthinkable. That they couldn't be expected to understand. She hardly understood it herself.

Her sense of relief began to leak away, to be replaced by a trembling uncertainty.

They would think her mad—be embarrassed, be hurt. *Hurt!* Especially Bess, to whom only a week ago she had stated firmly that she wasn't interested in men, didn't need a man in the way that Emma Porter's mother did. Bess would never trust her again, and she had built her relationship with her children on trust and love.

She felt herself slumping—mentally, physically, emotionally.

Something like despair washed over her. Whatever had made her think that she could get away with allowing herself to develop a friendship, an intimate friendship, with James Bruce? How could she have wept buckets on his chest this afternoon and allowed him to comfort her? Why hadn't she ignored all the warning signals—the vibes, the tenderness, the electricity charge—between them? If she hadn't responded to them he wouldn't have pressed her... would he?

Somehow she must find a way of extricating herself from the dinner date. It would be fatal to keep it. She would be lost if she did, unable to draw back. She wouldn't *want* to draw back. Her body, so long denied, was crying out to be loved and cherished, cared for. Impossible! Her heart ached unbearably.

Her head began to droop over the table and her nose

was almost on her plate when, with an exasperated snort, she jerked herself up straight. What the hell did her disappointment, her anguish—however deep—matter when her children's happiness was at stake?

'You all right, Mum?' asked Bess.

Kate grinned sheepishly. 'I'm fine, just a bit tired. We were busy in the MIU. I'm going to wash the dishes and then zonk out in front of the television.'

'Why don't you do that right now?' said Philip. 'We've finished our homework so we'll see to the dishes.'

'Well, if you're sure.'

'Pos-i-tive,' they crowed, as one.

She spent half the night lying awake and wondering how she was going to convince James that she couldn't have dinner with him on Friday or, indeed on any other night. She felt hollow inside, nauseated at the thought of it. She didn't know how, but she had to make it clear to him that from now on their relationship must be purely professional.

He must forget, they must both forget what had happened between them. It had been a mistake. They hadn't been drawn together by some mystical thread—that was an illusion. Call it anything—dismiss it as body chemistry, not something magical, extraordinary. That sort of thing only happened to teenagers, not to mature adults like themselves, and the sooner they recognised that the better.

She would gather up all her courage and tell James so tomorrow.

At last, exhausted and desperately unhappy, she drifted into a restless sleep, punctuated by a succession of dreams. Or rather one interrupted, but ongoing dream which she could only remember hazily as being frightening. The twins had been there—knee-high, small pigmy figures—looking up at her with tears streaming down their tiny faces, and she was bending down, down...

The dream always ended there, and each time she woke sweating, with tears streaming down her own face.

By five o'clock she'd had enough. She got up, showered, pulled on a track suit and jogged slowly down the drive across the almost deserted main road and onto the beach. Jogging was very therapeutic, she told herself sternly. It always made her feel better. She wouldn't think of her dream—she wouldn't think of anything. Blank.

The tide was out and there were acres of dark sand, gleaming wetly in the early morning sunshine just fingering its way across the bay through a pearly mist. It was only late May, but it was going to be another scorcher.

Burn weather, she thought, recalling the red-headed, fair-skinned girl who'd turned up for treatment yesterday. That was a mistake! Don't think about yesterday. Don't think about James, the kind, caring, confident doctor, the bewitching, gentle man.

'Get out of my head,' she groaned.

She put on a terrific spurt as she jogged eastwards toward the curving spit of land that embraced the bay about a mile away. Facing the rising sun, running fast along the shoreline and splashing through the shallow water helped chase his image away and empty her mind of demons.

By the time she reached the coastguard's cottage at the end of the spit and paused for a moment to look out across the bay she was calmer, more in charge of her thoughts. In the distance, rising out of the mist beyond the lighthouse, was the long wooden jetty that jutted out into the sea, marking the west end of the bay.

She loved this view, loved Millchester, her job, her loving, supportive parents and most of all her children. She was at peace with her world. Or she had been. And then James had arrived, and her peace had been shattered. James!

How the hell had he roused emotions in her that she had thought long dead—had wanted to be dead? She drew in a great shuddering breath. It didn't matter how but she must put him out of her mind and out of her *personal* life, for her children's sake. She would have to work amicably with him, but between them they would devise a formula for doing that so that the hospital didn't suffer.

She dreaded hurting him, seeing his warm hazel eyes go bleak. His hurt would be her hurt, but it was inevitable if she was not to hurt her children more and they were, and must be, her priority. Their happiness was in her hands.

Somehow she had to make that clear to him. Convince him that whatever they felt for and about each other she had a commitment that couldn't be ignored. Could an attractive, fancy-free bachelor, however kind and perceptive, appreciate that?

Not that it mattered whether he did or didn't, she thought unhappily. She would tell him today that their dinner date was off for there was nothing they had to discuss. The exquisite, fragile tenderness that had surfaced between them yesterday must be squashed as if it had never existed.

On this resolve she started out on her return journey at a much slower pace. But her heart pounded painfully and her breathing was laboured, and it had nothing to do with exercise. Just as the salt spray, whipped up by the slight breeze, had nothing to do with the tears that pricked the backs of her eyes.

But by the time she went on duty she had got herself well in hand, and her resolution to see James and deliver her ultimatum remained firm. Though resolving to see him and actually seeing him were two different things.

The had missed seeing each other when they first came on duty for, though she was early, James was already taking over from the night medical officer. And soon after her own arrival the night sister, June Brookes, appeared to make a lengthy report. Then for most of the morning she and James were working in different parts of the hospital and officially their paths didn't cross, though she briefly caught sight of him on her round.

He was operating in the day theatre unit on patients sent in by their GPs for minor surgery, and was performing a meniscectomy when Kate arrived in the unit. As she peeped through the viewing window of the door she glimpsed him, peering down an arthroscope at the injured knee.

'Dr Bruce been in there long?' she asked Janice Coleman, the sister in charge of the unit, when she made her way back through the recovery ward.

'He's only just started,' said Janice, 'so he'll be a while yet. He's got quite a few bods lined up—a couple of small lumpectomies, an oesophageal stretch, a varicose vein for sclerotherapy and a nasty carbuncle to finish with. Some of the local medics couldn't wait to hand over surgery to him—he has quite a reputation, I believe.'

'Yes, he's well qualified both as a physician and surgeon, and gained a lot of practical and, I gather, rather horrific experience overseas with aid agencies. According to the board, we're lucky to have netted him—he's quite a catch.'

'In more senses than one,' chuckled Janice. 'You'll have to watch your staff, Kate, with a lone bachelor out on the prowl. He's even charmed our Dora Cross, and that takes some doing. But, from what I've seen of him this morning, he's magic with the patients and that's what matters. Anyway, did you want to speak to him urgently? I could give him a message when he's finished the meniscectomy, and he could give you a buzz.'

'No, it's nothing important,' Kate fibbed airily, her heart thumping uncomfortably fast. 'It'll keep. You could tell him that I'll be having lunch in the canteen just after twelve, if he's free and would like to join me.'

'I'll tell him. He should be finished his list by then, and Dr Warner will take over. He's coming in to do a couple of his own patients and keep an eye on the rest.'

Kate was in the canteen by twelve. It was nearly empty, as she had guessed it would be at that early hour. None of the senior staff would be likely to turn up before twelve-thirty.

Like most things to do with the Memorial, the canteen food was surprisingly good, well prepared and presented by their own in house staff, and she usually enjoyed choosing whatever she fancied from the menu on offer. She was one of the small band of women who didn't need to diet to keep her figure. But today she couldn't have cared less what she ate and chose a simple salad from the glass-covered display, with stewed apple to follow in case she had to spin out the meal while she waited for James.

But she was still picking at her salad when he appeared, plonked a laden tray on the table and sat down opposite her.

He murmured, 'Hi Kate,' very softly, a wealth of tenderness in his voice.

'Hi,' She didn't dare look up and couldn't meet his eyes. Although she had been rehearsing all morning, she couldn't think what to say. Yet she must tell him. She gripped her knife and fork, unaware that her knuckles shone white. Her stomach churned.

James stared at her bowed head and longed to smooth her burnished hair and stroke her rigid hands—take her into his arms and comfort her. She was so tense. Something had happened, but what? What had occurred to spoil yesterday's magic?

His heart had turned somersaults when Sister had passed on the message that Kate wanted to see him in the canteen. He'd presumed that she was longing to see him as much as he was longing to see her as they'd not met that morning, yet here she was, seemingly afraid even to look at him. What had gone wrong in a few hours?

He could sense her retreating from him—his precious Katrina who had wept on his chest, her lovely violet-blue eyes drenched in tears. This woman whom he'd met a week ago, yet seemingly had known all his life, was going to reject him. He was damned if he was going to let that happen, not after all that had passed between them yesterday. *Never!*

They belonged together. He had never felt so sure about anything in his life, and he knew she felt the same. So she was devoted to her two young children. Well, of course she would be, should be—she was a natural loving mother. He wouldn't want it any different.

Obviously, it was this devotion, this commitment, that was tearing her to pieces now.

But it didn't have to be a stumbling block between them. He liked kids very much and generally formed a quick rapport with them, and could prove it if only she would give him the chance. And with *her* children it would be a labour of love and he would be patient, endlessly patient.

Keep cool, don't pressure her, he counselled himself. He leaned across the table, and said quietly, 'What's wrong, Kate? Anything I can do to help? You only have to say.' He waited but she didn't reply, just kept staring down at her plate and pushing the food around.

Give her time. James sat back, picked up a fork and

neatly twirled up a mouthful of pasta. He paused with it halfway to his mouth. 'Would I be right in thinking you're having second thoughts about us?' he asked after another minute's unbearable silence.

She raised her head and looked him straight in the eye. She nodded. 'Yes,' she said, in a clipped little voice. 'Only I've had my second thoughts and have reached a decision.'

'And that is?' He popped the pasta into his mouth and chewed it slowly. He knew, of course. She was going to tell him that it was all over between them before it had even got off the ground, that what had happened yesterday wasn't important. He could read it in her eyes—they were dark with pain and distress. Hell, it just wasn't true. She was denying herself as well as him and, what was worse, making it clear that it wasn't open for discussion.

'That I can't go out to dinner with you on Friday, James, or any other night. Our relationship must remain strictly professional.'

'Why?' he grated. He would damned well *make* her tell him, put it into words. He had meant to be so patient, but...

Her heart constricted at the sudden harshness in his voice. A flutter of anger blanketed out her pain for a moment. He sounded almost aggressive. She'd expected that he might try to argue her out of it but hadn't expected this belligerency, this bald—Why?

She said sharply, knowing it not to be true, 'It doesn't matter why—that's my business.'

He looked at her with smouldering, angry eyes. '*No*, you know that's nonsense. It's *our* business,' he rasped. 'For God's sake, Kate, let's be adult about this and talk. You owe me—us—that much. Don't dismiss this astonishing thing that's happened between us out of hand—it's too special for that.'

'There really isn't anything to talk about,' she said

wearily. 'I've thought it through, can't you see? It's because it's special that I have to stop it right now. It wouldn't be fair to my children. They're my priority and their happiness matters more to me than my happiness, or even yours, James.'

It hurt to say that. She tried to tell him with her eyes what she couldn't put into words, that what had happened was as precious to her as it was to him.

He stared at her in silence, his eyes full of pain as well as anger. She reached across the table, touched his hand, and murmured. 'I'm so sorry, James, so very, very sorry.' Then she scraped back her chair and fled from the canteen.

In a daze of unhappiness she worked her way through the afternoon, making an effort, with varying degrees of success, to banish all thoughts of James from her mind. She tried to forget that look in his eyes, forcing herself to concentrate on work.

She had several people to interview over the course of the afternoon—a trained nurse had applied to join the reserve pool, two young schoolgirls who wanted to learn about nursing as a career and were looking for holiday jobs during much of July and August and a middle-aged woman, recently widowed and needing to supplement her pension and do something useful at the same time.

Rose Johnson, the qualified nurse, didn't take long to interview. She was a bright, vivacious forty-four-year-old whose three children were now all at college.

'Now I can't wait to get back to nursing,' she told Kate enthusiastically. 'I couldn't all the time my husband was in the navy because he was away too much, but now he's retired and is working in electronics and he's all in favour of me nursing again.'

Her references were excellent. She had already arranged to do the statutory refresher course, and was very willing to attend the Memorial's own in-house training and assessment days, before being appointed under contract.

'Everyone joining the permanent staff has to attend these,' explained Kate, 'so that newcomers understand exactly what is expected of them. We look for high standards and good old-fashioned tender loving care to all patients at all times. Anyone not willing to comply is out. You'll find working conditions here first rate, and we expect you to reciprocate in kind by giving a hundred per cent dedication. Any problems, you can always come and see me—my door's always open.'

'Sounds exactly what I'm looking for,' said Rose as she got up to leave. 'TLC doesn't seem to be a priority in some hospitals these days—everything seems to be so high-tech—but I think it's terribly important.'

'Here, it's the prime virtue,' replied Kate, warmed by her enthusiasm. 'Good luck with your refresher course next week. Look forward to having you aboard in a month's time.'

The two schoolgirls were also enthusiastic.

One dark, one fair, Zoe Tucker and Belinda Wright were pretty girls of almost seventeen. The fair Belinda looked vaguely familiar to Kate. They had done quite well in their GCSEs and were now studying for their A levels, but thought they might switch to a vocational qualification course if this would lead them into nursing as a career.

'Stick to your A levels,' advised Kate, 'since you know what you want to do, and start your nurse training proper with the best grades you can get.'

Would there be a chance of working at the Memorial in some nursing capacity during the summer holidays? they wanted to know.

'So that we can get the *feel* of working in a hospital,' explained Zoe, beaming at Kate. 'My nan's a nurse, or she was. She's retired now, but she says this is important.'

'She's absolutely right,' agreed Kate. 'Is she pleased that you're interested in nursing?'

'Over the moon,' said Zoe. 'Says it's the best job in the world if you're cut out for it.'

'And you think you are?' asked Kate, returning her smile.

'Definitely,' replied Zoe.

'And what about you, Belinda? Have you any nursing connections?'

'No, not nursing, exactly,' said Belinda shyly. 'But my mum's a chiropodist. She visits here sometimes to treat patients. She suggested that we tried here for a job. She reckons this is the best hospital there is.'

Recognition dawned. 'Oh, of course, you're Marie Wright's daughter. How interesting.' Kate looked thoughtfully at the two girls. 'So both of you have some idea of what nursing might be like and understand that it's hard work and that you have to be prepared to do all sorts jobs, not all of them pleasant.'

They nodded vigorously.

Kate made up her mind. They were material worth nurturing. 'Right, then, ladies, if your school references are satisfactory we'll give you a trial as temporary junior assistant helpers. If you wait outside for a moment my secretary, Mrs Hill, will see you. She'll give you application forms to fill in and explain about uniforms and so on.' She stood up and shook hands. 'See you both at the end of July,' she said.

Beaming with pleasure and bubbling their thanks, the girls jostled each other out of the room.

Kate buzzed Maggie Hill, her part-time secretary, on the intercom.

'Maggie, these two girls I've just been interviewing look very promising. Give them all the gen and arrange for them to start in July. And send in this other lady you've got lined up for me, please.'

'Will do,' said Maggie, 'but I've got a message here from Dr Bruce. He'd like you to ring him as soon as possible—he's in his office. Will you do that before you see Mrs Day?'

Kate trembled and her heart knocked against her ribs. Just to hear his voice... She took a deep, steadying breath. 'No, I'll phone him later,' she said. 'Just send in Mrs Day.'

'But—' began Maggie.

'Now, please,' Kate interrupted, and switched off the intercom.

From the moment she entered the office it was obvious to Kate that the widowed Mrs Joan Day was not a well women. She was tall, thin, agitated and pale except for her cheeks which were stained bright red, making her look like a painted doll. Her handshake was hot, limp and moist, her pale blue protuberant eyes were glazed as she was frowning as if in pain. She had said that she was fifty, but looked much older.

'Do sit down,' invited Kate.

Mrs Day didn't sit, but held onto the back of the chair. 'Sorry, I shouldn't have come—wasting your time,' she said in a quavery voice. 'I've got a terrible headache.' She closed her eyes and swayed alarmingly.

Kate jumped up, sped round the desk and caught Mrs Day as her knees crumpled. She lowered the older woman gently to the floor.

'Feel giddy,' mumbled Mrs Day.

'Close your eyes and lie still,' said Kate. 'You'll feel

better in a moment.' She knelt down beside the recumbent woman who was almost panting, taking in light, shallow, rapid breaths. She felt at Mrs Day's wrist for her radial pulse. It was huge, bounding and very erratic, alternately skipping beats and speeding up.

All Kate's instincts and training were on the alert. Probably severe hypertension, she thought. Bet her blood pressure's sky-high—could be brewing up a stroke. She stood up, leaned over the desk and switched on the intercom.

Her secretary answered at once.

In a low voice Kate explained, 'Maggie, I have a little problem here. Mrs Day has collapsed. It's not an emergency, but let Dr Bruce know and then nip along to Medical and fetch a BP set and a couple of pillows.'

'Rightio, will do.' Like the perfect secretary she was, Maggie didn't ask any questions.

Kate returned to her kneeling position and continued to reassure the agitated woman while she monitored her pulse, which remained alarmingly bounding and uneven even though she had been resting for a few minutes.

Mrs Day opened her eyes suddenly and stared at Kate with a frightened expression. 'I'm sorry, Sister,' she whispered, 'giving you all this trouble. I'll be all right in a minute and then I'll be able to go home.'

Not, thought Kate, if your blood pressure's anything like as high as I think it is. 'Has this happened before?' she asked gently.

'Yes, a couple of times. This thumping headache comes on and then I feel giddy, but if I lie down for a little while it goes off.'

'Have you seen your doctor about it?'

'No, we'd only just moved here when my husband died.' Her eyes filled with tears, and she said jerkily, 'I'd had enough of doctors. I thought it was down to the shock and because I'm lonely and that if I got a job I'd feel better, but now—Oh. . .' Her eyes swivelled past Kate and her voice trailed off as the door opened, and James's large form filled the doorway.

He flicked an infinitely tender look at Kate, and her heart lurched. He's forgiven me for hurting him, she thought, and she felt as if a tremendous burden had been lifted from her as a great wave of longing—of love—for this gentle giant of a man washed over her.

'Can I help, Sister?'

'Please, Doctor.' She tried to convey with her eyes that his message had been received and understood.

It was. His mouth lifted at the corners and he inclined his head slightly, then he crossed the room in a few long strides and crouched down beside the recumbent Mrs Day.

'Hello there,' he said, in the quiet, comforting manner that patients found instantly reassuring. 'I'm Dr Bruce. Sister's asked me to have a look at you. Apparently you virtually collapsed at her feet.' He smiled, slid his fingers round her wrist and began taking her pulse. 'So, how are you feeling now, Mrs Day?'

Her pinched lips trembled. 'Better, thanks, Doctor. Not so giddy. Lying flat's helped—it always does—but I'd like to sit up a bit now, if I may.'

As if on cue, Maggie arrived with the pillows and the sphygmomanometer. 'Anything I can do?' she asked as she handed them over to Kate who met her in the doorway.

Kate mouthed softly, 'You could alert Women's Med that we'll probably need a bed for an emergency admission presently, and have a nurse and a porter standing by with a wheelchair.'

Maggie's eyebrows shot up. 'That bad?'

'I think so. I'll let you know as soon as Dr Bruce has finished his examination.

As Kate had predicted, James found that Joan Day's blood pressure was very high and all the signs indicated that she was in imminent danger of having a stroke, heart failure or kidney failure if it wasn't treated. In addition to this, he suspected from her history and his brief examination that she might also be suffering from a hyperactive thyroid, but that would have to be confirmed.

He explained his findings gently, but with his usual frankness, and then added, 'So we need to have you in for a week or so, Mrs Day, to do various tests and start you on medication immediately.'

'You mean today?'

'Today.' He was firm.

'But I've nothing with me—nightdress, toothbrush—and there's no one at home...' Tears began to roll down her cheeks.

Kate put a comforting arm round her thin shoulders. 'That's not a problem, love. We can arrange for someone to pick up your things and, meanwhile, Ward Sister will fix you up with a nightdress. Right now it's important that we get you into bed because what you most need is rest.'

A few minutes later a ward nurse and a porter arrived with a wheelchair, and a somewhat reassured Mrs Day was wheeled away along the corridor to Dorothy Lang, the women's medical ward.

CHAPTER SEVEN

THE office seemed strangely quiet and empty after the bustling activity packed into the last half hour or so and, finding herself alone with James, Kate felt suddenly and inexplicably shy.

He was standing just inside the door which he had closed behind the departing patient and escorts, and was surveying her steadily with his warm, brown-flecked, hazel-green eyes. But Kate could read nothing in them and hadn't a clue what he was thinking.

Did he want to her to refer to the silent messages they had exchanged with such gentle fervour a little while before, or did he want her to ignore the ecstatic, intimate exchange? Forget it? Could she possibly be mistaken in what she thought she'd read in them?

In a breathy rush, for something to say to break the small silence that had descended upon them, she said, 'Poor Mrs Day, coming for an interview for a job and ending up as a patient.'

James accepted Kate's neutral remark at face value and, sensing her uncertainty and wanting to put her at ease, he squashed the desire to take her in his arms and reassure her with kisses and said, in a dry professional manner. 'More accurate perhaps to say lucky Mrs Day to have collapsed in your office, Kate, and not alone at home. She's a very sick woman and urgently in need of a lot of care and medication, and right now I must take myself off and get something organised.'

Of course, he was quite right. The patient had to come

first—quite proper—but Kate's heart plunged. She wanted to hear him say what she thought he'd said earlier with his eyes. She didn't want him to go, not yet, not without saying something.

He half opened the door, paused and added softly, 'As for you and I, Kate, you know we have to talk with no more prevaricating, whatever you said at lunchtime. As far as I'm concerned, Friday night's still on. I'll pick you up as agreed at seven-thirty. Be ready, my love, and don't worry—all's going to be well, promise you.'

'*My love!*' His love! Her heart lifted and thumped a joyful tattoo loud in her ears.

'But—'

'No buts, Kate. I'll be at the lodge on Friday at seven-thirty.' He smiled suddenly, a wide, tender smile that lifted the corners of his mouth. He touched his fingers to his lips, whisked his large frame neatly through the open doorway and disappeared into the corridor.

Vividly, however hard she tried to concentrate, that loving smile haunted her as she worked her way through the next hour or so on automatic pilot and, try as she might, she couldn't dispel it. Every few minutes she found herself staring into space with an inane grin in her face. And his words—'my love'—spoken so gently with that faint Scottish burr, teased as her too, and she prickled all over with a deep, satisfying pleasure.

It didn't help that she was virtually chained to the office for the afternoon, reading and signing letters and tapping out orders for equipment and drugs. Fulfilling these mundane paper tasks gave her too much time to think, to mull over all that had happened since she had jogged along the sands in the early morning sunshine.

The unhappiness that had swamped her then and

immediately after her confrontation with James in the canteen had completely vanished, replaced by a mixture of euphoria and detached bewilderment as she tried to assimilate the seesawing emotions of the day.

That she would meet with James on Friday she now accepted as a forgone conclusion. He was dead right. They couldn't ignore what had occurred between them, this astonishing happening that had drawn and held them together, overwhelmed them—two practical, mature people. They had to discuss it, decide what to do about it. Though what that might be, she had no idea. Everything had happened so quickly, taking her by surprise, that she was still in shock. It was unbelievable that they had met only a little over a week ago.

So they would meet the talk, but deep inside herself she knew that all the talking in the world wouldn't alter the way she felt about James. It was something primitive and beautiful that had hit her—both of them—out of the blue, and it was here to stay. It just wasn't going to go away. She knew this just as certainly as she knew that her children's happiness must come first and that absolutely nothing and nobody was going to jeopardise that.

But did her love for her children *have* to conflict with her love for James? She began to wonder, tentatively at first and then with a little flare of hope, if she might enter into some sort of satisfactory relationship with James which Bess and Philip would find acceptable.

The idea took her by surprise. How this might be achieved she wasn't sure, but she *was* sure that whatever it was it would involve patience and, initially, compromise. Would James be willing to go along with that?

Willing, yes, of course he would be! No question about it. He was so positive that all would be well, and had seemed so confident, but—

The intercom buzzed. Kate flipped a switch and Maggie's voice came over loud and clear. 'Don't forget you've arranged to see Grace at a quarter to five,' she reminded Kate, 'to have a conflab about staffing during the holiday period.'

Kate said, 'Oh, Lord, I had forgotten.' She looked at her watch. 'The twins should be home by now. Give me a line through to the lodge, Maggie, and I'll have a word with them.'

'OK, you have it,' said Maggie.

Bess answered the phone. 'Hi, Mum, you're not going to be late, are you?'

'No, should be home before six. Why, something important on?'

'The tide's coming in and we thought we'd go for a swim tonight before supper. It's so hot, and the bus was simply boiling—we're all yucky and sticky.'

'OK, I'll join you for just a quick dip, but not for long. The water's still freezing, though I know you two don't seem to notice.'

'You don't have to come, Mum. We could go on our own and be back before you get home.'

Kate hesitated for a moment, then said quietly, 'You know I'd rather you didn't.'

Bess snorted noisily and said in a resigned tone of voice, 'It's not fair, Mum, we're not babies. We're not going to do anything stupid, but if that's the way you want it... But, please, please, don't be late—promise?'

'Promise.'

'Do you think,' Kate asked Grace half an hour later when they'd finished their discussion about staffing levels, 'that I'm too protective of Bess and Philip?'

Grace frowned. 'Occasionally, perhaps, but on the

whole, no. They're a credit to you, Kate, sensible and independent. You're very loving, and loving and protecting go in tandem, but there's nothing wrong with that, provided one keeps the protective bit in perspective. Quite the contrary. Why do you ask?'

'I don't like them going swimming on their own. They know that, and have always accepted it. But Bess was a bit bolshie about it just now when I said they had to wait till I get home to do this evening. Perhaps it is silly. They're both good swimmers, but I just feel I ought to be there.'

'Not surprising. Understandable. You can't help thinking of the bods who get into difficulties in the water and turn up in the MIU half-drowned. That's the trouble with doctors and nurses—you only see the worst side of things. Be positive and think of all the folk who don't end up in hospital, not the handful of people who do.'

'Yes. I know it's ridiculous. They're nearly always visitors, unused to the tides and ignoring warning signs, and I know Bess and Philip wouldn't do that—they understand about these things.' She pulled a face and sat up very straight. 'Grace, I've been a fool. May I use your phone?'

'Be my guest.'

Kate phoned the lodge, and this time Philip answered.

He groaned when he heard it was Kate. 'Does this mean you *are* going to be late and we can't go swimming?'

'No,' said Kate, firming up her voice, 'I'll be home by six, as promised, but I've had a rethink. If you and Bess want to go on without me, please do, just take care. I'll meet you on the beach later.'

Philip whistled through his teeth. 'Gosh, you sure, Mum?'

'Positive,' she said, smartly replacing the receiver.

'Well done,' said Grace. 'Good thinking. You've done the right thing. They're good kids, and they'll appreciate being responsible for themselves. But I can imagine that it wasn't an easy decision to make.'

'No, but thanks for helping me see things straight. You're quite right, I've just got to accept that my children are growing up and simply do not need me to protect them all the time.'

'I suppose,' mused Grace thoughtfully, 'though I have no personal experience of parenting, that this is how children learn how to deal with the slings and arrows, as good old Shakespeare put it.'

'Yes, I suppose it is,' said Kate, equally thoughtfully. 'Parents have to let go, but still be around to pick up the pieces and not say I told you so when things go wrong.'

'Awesome,' said Grace, with raised eyebrows. 'Rather you than me. That's something I couldn't take on board.'

Would James, Kate thought when she returned to her office a little later, also think, as a bachelor, that it was too awesome and difficult to taken on board? Would he accept that loving her would mean loving her children, sharing her with them?

She went off duty in good time, but was determined not to let herself hurry. She was *not*, she told herself, going to rush down to the beach and check on the kids. She would let them see that she trusted them completely. She sauntered down to the lodge, and changed in a leisurely fashion into shorts, a loose cotton shirt and thonged sandals.

It was after six when she made her way, deep in muddled thought, across the wide, busy coast road and onto the sands. She knew that this decision to start being less protective on a purely physical plane was only a beginning, and that Grace's words about keeping things in perspective would subtly alter her relationship with her children. It was about to enter a new phase. Would it help them to accept a future that would include James? Her heart turned over. Would that it might.

There were still a few people scattered around on the beach but not many in the water, except for one or two small children, paddling in the shallows.

Kate shielded her eyes against the glare that bounced back from the water and spotted Bess and Philip swimming a little way off shore, their bright fair heads bobbing rhythmically up and down. After a moment they caught sight of her and waved. She waved back, then made her way to where they'd left their distinctive bright towels draped over the nearest groyne.

She sat down facing the evening sun, leaned back against the rough wood of the groyne and closed her eyes. The rhythmic, sibilant surging of the sea as it rippled up the gentle slope of the shore should have soothed her tumultuous thoughts, but it didn't. Her mind continued to seethe with unanswerable questions.

How was she going to begin to reconcile this explosion of love for James, a love that was not going to go away, with her long-term loving relationship with her children?

For how long would she be able to conceal the depth of her feelings for James, put up the pretence of pursuing a friendship only? For how long could she bear to deceive—or try to protect—her children?

Her earlier uncertainties resurfaced and, no longer comforted by James's reassurances, she pulled her eyebrows together in a ferocious frown. She must think—be sensible. . .

A shower of cold water spattered over her warm skin. She opened her eyes wide. The twins were standing at her feet and smiling down at her, water glistening on their golden tanned skin. Her frown disappeared and she smiled back at them.

'Hi, Mum,' they said in unison.

'Hi, yourselves. Had a good swim?' She reached behind her for their towels. 'Here, wrap up—you must be freezing.'

'Course we're not,' said Philip, towelling himself vigorously. 'It was fab.'

Bess wrapped her towel round her shoulders and sat down beside Kate, her pretty little face suddenly serious. 'Why did you decide to let us go on our own, Mum?'

'Because I suddenly realised that you're growing up and were quite capable of—'

There was a piercing shriek from a small boy, splashing in the shallows a few yards away. He was staring down at one foot, which he had lifted out of the water. It was pouring with bright red blood.

In the seconds it took Kate to reach him tears started streaming down his face and he was sobbing hysterically as he wobbled on his one good foot. Making reassuring noises, she scooped him clear of the water and, oblivious of the blood flowing freely down her her shirt and shorts, began to carry him up the sandy beach.

Philip and Bess ran forward to meet her. 'What can we do, Mum?'

'Wrap a towel round his foot, but not too tightly in case there's some glass or whatever in the cut, and spread out the other towel so that I can lay him down on it.'

With more soothing words, Kate placed the child, whose noisy sobs had dropped to a whisper, on the towel. 'You hold his hand and talk to him. Bess. Find out his name,' she said, 'and who he's with it you can. And, Philip, you lift up his leg and hold it steady while I examine his foot.

We'll have it well up for a few minutes to help reduce the bleeding.'

Philip raised the boy's leg nearly vertically. 'How's that?' he asked.

'Fine.' Kate unwound the bulky towel. The outer layers were dry, but beneath it was already saturated and blood was still oozing sluggishly from a long, deep cut in the boy's foot, running along the sole from toes to heel. But it was clean, sliced by something smooth and sharp. 'Needs clever stitching,' she murmured, 'and the ligaments and nerves will have to be checked for damage.'

She refolded the towel and wrapped it firmly round the foot. 'We'll have to take him up to the MIU, but we can hardly do that till we find whoever's supposed to be looking after him. Any luck with his name, Bess?'

Bess shook her head. 'He doesn't seem to know,' she said softly, and gave the boy, who was half sitting up and leaning against her, a hug.

'I want my mummy,' whimpered the boy, burrowing his head into Bess's side.

'Is Mummy with you on the beach, love?' Kate asked.

'Yes,' he snuffled, and the whimper rose to a wail. 'Mummy, Mummy.'

Kate looked round. Their part of the beach stretched emptily away to the next groyne.

Philip peered over the groyne behind them. 'There's someone over there,' he said. 'Asleep or sunbathing. Shall I go and see if that's his mother? There's no one else about.'

'Yes,' said Kate, in a low voice through tight lips, 'and if it is get her here on the double before this child has a fit. Some mother—I can't believe she hasn't heard this racket.'

Philip leapt over the groyne and sped across the sand,

returning a few minutes later with a wide-eyed, frightened young woman beside him.

'This is Tony's mother,' he said. 'Susie West.'

Ignoring Kate and Bess, the young woman, who looked little more than a girl in her teens, flung herself down beside the boy, hugged him tight and burst into tears. 'Oh, Tone, what've you done?' she mumbled.

Seeing that she was so young and obviously distressed, Kate, who had been prepared to tear her off a strip, confined herself to saying curtly, 'Cut himself badly on something sharp so we'll have to take him up to the hospital to have some stitches put in.'

Susie shuddered and muttered tearfully, 'Hospital! Does he have to go in? I don't like hospitals. It was horrible when I had to go in when I had Tone—big and kind of scary.'

Kate said gently, 'This one won't scare you. It's small, just across the road and I work there. I'm the nursing sister in charge.'

'Will you come with us, then?'

'Of course. I'll go ahead to fetch my car so I can drive you up to the hospital. You make your way up slowly and wait for me at the top of the beach. Bess and Philip will look after you.'

She flicked a smile at the twins. 'That OK with you?'

They nodded and smiled back at her. 'Fine, Mum,' said Philip. 'We'll take care of things.'

'Don't cross the road. I'll come over to fetch you. Wait by the bollards.'

Leaving them to sort themselves out, Kate hurried up the beach. The coast road was still busy, and it took her a few minutes to negotiate her way through the traffic and cross to the hospital entrance.

The lodge stood some hundred yards inside the entrance.

She spurted up the slope and had almost almost reached it when a car rounded a bend in the drive, cruising slowly down from the direction of the hospital. An elderly, aristocratic, dark blue Rover saloon.

James!

A huge wave of pleasure surged through her as she saw him approaching. Wonderful. It was so good to see him. She needed him, and he was there.

She stopped in the middle of the drive and waved her arms about like a windmill. He couldn't miss her. He put on a terrific burst of speed and skidded to an abrupt halt a few yards from her.

'Kate, what the hell's happened?' he called through the open window as the car came to a standstill. 'My God, you're covered in blood.' He threw open the door and leapt out, reached her in a few long strides and swept her into his arms. 'Are you hurt, love?' he asked, low-voiced, urgent.

She had forgotten her bloodstained clothes. She said breathlessly, savouring his concern and his arms about her, 'No. I'm fine. There's a boy on the beach, cut foot, needs stitching. His mother's with him and the twins. I came up to get my car.'

James kissed her hard on the mouth, and released her. 'We'll take mine,' he said, propelling her gently before him towards the stately Rover.

An hour later, bathed in mellow evening sunlight, they stood outside the minor injuries unit which had closed its doors for the night. Patients and staff had gone home. They were the last to leave.

Except for James's car, the MIU car park was empty. They were alone, isolated from the rest of the world, thought Kate. From round the corner, out of sight, came the sound of cars coming and going in the main car park. Visiting time. It emphasised their isolation. They looked at each other, conscious of a feeling of *déjà vu*, reminded of those few minutes alone in Kate's office that afternoon when it had suddenly emptied of other people.

Now, as then, it was Kate who broke the silence. And now, as then, she felt strangely shy at finding herself alone with him.

'That was a neat bit of fancy stitching you did on young Tony,' she said, a trifle breathlessly.

She was aware that he knew that she was playing for time, putting off the moment of intimacy.

'Thank you.' He inclined his head in a laconic little bow. 'I'm a dab hand at embroidery.' His wide mouth curved into another of his all-embracing smiles.

Touched by the sun, his hazel eyes gleamed more gold than green. They were full of tenderness and laughter as they swept over her from head to toe.

'You're a bloody mess,' he said. He flicked a finger at a large red blob on her shirt. 'A beautiful, bloody mess, Katrina Brown. I'd better get you home back to your bright, handsome kids.' He took her hand and squeezed it. 'I'm so glad that I've met them, though it was necessarily brief under the circumstances.'

Katrina! A true Scotsman, he rolled the R lovingly. It sounded so right, coming from him. And he thought the children bright and handsome. What had they thought of him? It had been a kerbside introduction as they'd loaded Tony and Mrs West into the car. 'This is Bess and Philip—this is Dr Bruce.'

'Hi, Dr Bruce,' Philip had replied cheerfully, followed by a rather shy greeting from Bess, who had blushed slightly.

'Smiling, James had replied, 'Nice to meet you both.'

They had exchanged quick polite handshakes.

James squeezed her hand again, recalling her to the present. 'We've broken the ice, Kate, that's important—to them, to us. We must follow it up as soon as possible. I want to get to know them better.'

He was right. As usual, she thought wryly. Squashing all caution, she said impulsively, 'Take pot luck and come and have supper with us—beans on toast or salad or something. I haven't had time to prepare anything today.'

'I *love* beans on toast,' he said, and bent to kiss her on the lips, firmly, possessively.

Kate's imagination ran riot on the short drive down from the MIU to the lodge. She must have been mad to have invited James to supper without warning, this man with whom she had a remarkable rapport yet hardly knew. She agonised. How was she going to introduce him for a second time? What were they going to talk about all the evening? Supposing Bess and Philip didn't like him?

James parked the car on the grass verge in front of the lodge and turned to look at her. 'Nervous?' he asked with a smile.

'Yes.'

'Well, don't be. It's going to be all right.'

'How can you be so sure?'

'Instinct,' he said firmly. 'Women don't have the monopoly on instinct. We'll hit it off famously, you'll see. Come on, out you get and lead the way.'

Bess was crouching down to attend to a dish in the oven and Philip was out of sight, fetching something from the walk-in larder, when they reached the kitchen door so their arrival went unnoticed.

Then Kate stepped over the threshold and Bess said, without looking up, 'Supper won't be long, Mum. Thought we'd have that vegetable lasagne that you made the other day.' She straightened up, turned and saw James. Her pretty face was shiny and pink from the heat. She beamed. 'Oh. . . Dr Bruce, how lovely. Have you come to supper? There's masses of lasagne.'

James laughed. 'And to think your mother promised me baked beans on toast,' he said.

Philip bobbed out of the larder. He grinned. 'Hello again, Dr Bruce. I promise you'll find Mum's lasagne a touch more exotic than baked beans. It's brilliant.' He hesitated a moment, and then said, 'Would you like a lager? There's some in the fridge.'

'Thank you, I'd love one.'

'Mum, do you want one, or would you rather have a glass of wine?'

Her eleven-year-old son seemed to have slipped into the role of the perfect host with consummate ease.

Kate blinked. She was staggered. That the children would be polite and friendly she took for granted, but the warmth and ease of their welcome to someone whom they'd only just met surprised her. For a fleeting, bizarre moment she wondered if they guessed that he was special to her. But of course they couldn't know that.

Philip said, 'Well, Mum, what's it to be?'

She pulled herself together. 'Oh, nothing for the moment. I must go and get changed.'

'Yes, you do look pretty gruesome,' said Bess with a huge grin. 'Go on, Mum, you get cleaned up and we'll look after Dr Bruce.'

'Oh, thanks,' said Kate, further rattled by the cool confidence of her daughter, 'I'll leave you to it.' With a mumbled apology to James and a promise not to be long, she fled upstairs.

She would have loved a shower, but made do with

splashing her face and arms with cold water, spraying herself lavishly with her favourite perfume and putting on a touch of make-up. In record time she changed into a cream cotton wrap-around skirt and a silky bronze vest top that matched her shining hair and hooked on a pair of amber drop earrings.

Would Bess and Philip think her a bit dressed up for supper? Did she look all right? Would James approve? She hoped he would.

It was clear that he did. He was sitting at the table in animated discussion with the twins when she sailed into the kitchen, but broke off in mid-sentence, rose to his feet and pulled out the chair beside him.

His eyes, full of admiration, swept over her. 'You look absolutely—great,' he said, longing to say more, unable to keep the warm admiration out of his voice. She gave him a startled warning look, and he added lightly with a laugh, 'Much less bloody.'

'So you do,' agreed Philip. 'Now, what are you going to have, Mum, wine or lager?'

'Oh, wine, please. Pour it out, but I'll dish up first.'

Bess scraped her chair back. 'No, you won't,' she said, in the no-nonsense tone that Kate herself sometimes used. 'I'm going to do that—you just sit down and relax.'

Kate stared at her daughter, always sensible and helpful but suddenly so crisply cool and confident, so...so grown-up.

She said uncertainly, 'Well, if you're sure.'

'That sounds like an order to me,' said James with a laugh. 'Why don't you do as your capable daughter suggests, Kate, and let her manage? Come on, do as you're told—sit down and relax.'

* * *

For the rest of the evening she did just that. She felt bemused and detached and let the conversation swirl and eddy about her, contributing the occasional remark. But for most part she was content to watch and listen, wondering at the ease with which these three people whom she loved were connecting with each other. They seemed to be able to talk together about anything and everything, as if they had known each other for years.

She breathed in sharply. Her heart gave a joyful leap. How wonderful if... Her thoughts took flight, and she stared unseeingly before her.

James whispered in her ear, 'Come back to earth, Kate.'

She heard him from a distance, floated down from the clouds, turned her head slowly and met his smiling eyes. Alarm bells jangled... Philip and Bess... They were at the kitchen end of the large, old-fashioned kitchen-breakfast room beyond the divider worktop, arguing amicably and noisily as Philip washed up and Bess made coffee.

Kate hadn't even realised that they'd finished supper, though she vaguely remembered eating rhubarb and custard.

Blood rushed to her cheeks and receded—she seemed to have missed out on most of the meal. She dredged up a smile. 'Sorry about that, so rude. I don't know what got into me—I was sort of daydreaming.' She looked anxiously in the twins' direction.

'They didn't notice,' murmured James. 'You said yes and no in all the right places.' He laughed softly. 'Was it a nice daydream Kate? Was I in it?'

Her cheeks flared red again, but she was spared having to answer as Bess rang out, 'Coffee's up.' She appeared round the divider with a tray, bearing two aromatic steaming cups, which she placed on the table between them. She passed a cup to James, and indicated the sugar bowl and milk jug. 'Do help yourself, Dr Bruce.'

'Thank you, Bess, but I like it black.'

Philip was still clattering around with the dishes.

Bess sighed dramatically. 'I suppose I'd better go and do the drying-up for him,' she said, and waltzed back to the other end of the room.

'Don't be long,' Kate called after her. 'You two should be thinking about bed.'

'What time's bed?' asked James.

Was he pretending to be interested because he knew it would please her, or was he just making polite conversation, humouring her? Why couldn't she talk to him freely and easily, as the children had done?

She frowned and shrugged. 'Well, it's a bit elastic, especially in the summer. Usually between half past nine and ten.'

Suddenly she longed for the strange evening to be at an end. Longed to be on her own to think. She felt drained. 'You shouldn't,' she said regressively, pouring milk liberally into her own cup, 'drink coffee black at this time of night.' She glanced at the wall clock—a quarter to ten.

James's eyes twinkled and his lips twitched at the corners. He'd seen through her ruse to get rid of him, but obviously didn't resent it. Perceptive as he was, he probably understood that she needed to be alone.

'You're quite right, all that undiluted caffeine—lethal.' He topped his cup up with milk and took a couple of sips. 'Time I was going, Kate. It's been a long day. Thanks for a super supper and a stimulating evening.'

She must be polite. She murmured, 'Sorry I was so—'

'Think nothing of it. Your children kept me entertained—they're great company.' he stood up.

Bess and Philip bounced up from the other end of the room.

'Do you have to go?' asked Philip.

'Afraid I do. Busy day tomorrow—early start in Theatre. I need my beauty sleep. And your mother looks dead on her feet. I'm sure she needs hers.' He smiled down at her and for one startling moment Kate thought he was going to kiss her, there in front of Bess and Philip.

She said abruptly, 'You don't have to go through the kitchen—you can go out this way,' She rose and led the way through an arch into a tiny hall. She opened the front door, giving onto the honeysuckle-hung porch.

The sky to the west was streaked purple, raspberry red and a delicate almond green. A faint breeze stirred the pine trees. A sliver of moon and a single star quivered above them in the twilit sky. The coast road was quiet.

They escorted him to his car, tucked away behind the hedge.

James breathed in deeply. 'Beautiful night,' he said. 'A fitting end to a delightful evening. Goodnight to you all and, again, my thanks for making me so welcome.' He lowered himself into the driving seat, and added softly, 'See you tomorrow, Kate.'

They watched him drive off into the purple dusk. Bess slipped her arm through Kate's. 'He's nice, Mum, isn't he? No wonder you like working with him.'

'Yes,' said Kate, making the understatement of the year. 'He *is* rather nice.'

CHAPTER EIGHT

THOUGH James had promised to see Kate on Thursday as he had taken leave of her at the lodge, they did not, in fact, meet up. He was busy operating in Theatre and Kate, who usually popped in and out of the surgical ward on operating days, was at the other end of the hospital, covering for an absent sister on the long stay unit.

Neither did their paths cross at work on Friday, except when they greeted each other in Reception as they arrived on duty—and even that was interrupted by the night medic who wanted James's opinion on a post-operative patient.

It was frustrating, thought Kate resignedly as the day wore on and she still saw nothing of him, but it was all par for the course. That was medicine. But please don't let anything prevent us having dinner together tonight, she prayed silently.

Her prayers were answered when James arrived promptly at seven-thirty, drawing up with neat precision on the grass verge beside the hedge.

Kate, who was waiting for him in the garden, abstractedly deadheading the few early roses that had already blossomed and died in the late May heatwave, made herself stroll casually across to the gate to greet him. She felt incredibly nervous, as nervous as a teenager on a first date not a responsible mother with two eleven-year-old children. Would he kiss her—wouldn't he kiss her—did she want him to?

She had been in a state of uncertainty ever since she

had come off duty, spending a long time over the make-up and vacillating over what to wear. She plumped eventually for an old favourite—a sleeveless Chinese-style, satin-finished cotton dress, ice blue patterned with tiny red flowers and a stiff mandarin collar. With plain gold drop earrings, strappy dark blue sandals and a soft mohair stole draped round her shoulders, it made a cool, sophisticated ensemble which went some way towards boosting her morale.

Her morale was further boosted when James thrust the gate open and strode towards her with his arms outstretched, making no attempt to conceal his admiration. 'Oh, my dear, lovely Katrina,' he said, rolling the R sensuously. He took her hands in his and held her at arm's length. 'You look stunningly beautiful. Very Oriental, inscrutable and mystical.' His eyes, full of tenderness and teasing laughter, devoured her, but he didn't kiss her.

Don't be fazed—think of something to say, Kate told herself. She said huskily, 'Sorry I haven't got my crystal ball with me.'

He chuckled. 'Not to worry, crystal balls are out this season—very unfashionable.' He squeezed her hands and drew her to him so that she had to tilt her face to look up at him. He said softly, 'And I don't need a crystal ball to tell me that I'm going to kiss you.'

Kate's heart hammered away like mad. A car swished up the drive. 'Visiting time,' she murmured. 'Somebody might see us over the hedge.'

James grinned. 'We're off duty, Sister Brown.' He brushed his lips across the tip of her nose. 'Relax, love. For once forget about the damned hospital and let yourself go. It's just a little kiss. I won't even spoil your make-up.' Bending his head, he kissed her firmly but gently on her parted lips.

'Oh!' The kiss surprised her by its brevity and lack of passion. It wasn't what she'd expected. It was the kiss of a friend, not that of the man who had rocketed into her life and proclaimed his love for her in the space of ten days. Having told her to relax, it was as if he was holding back. Why? And was she glad or sorry? She stared at him with a puzzled frown.

He held her lightly by the shoulders, and said quietly, 'You don't want to be rushed, do you, Kate? Quite right. Neither do I. We've got a lot of talking to do yet. In spite of being struck by lightning, we need time to adjust and to learn about each other and our various commitments. A period of courtship, to use an old-fashioned but apt phrase.'

She liked the sound of an old-fashioned courtship, a breathing space between the unreality of falling head over heels in love and the practicalities of everyday life. Practicalities! The twins—did James consider them as part of this period of adjustment?

A trifle uncertainty, she said, 'Not just us—the children, James, I have to think of Bess and Philip. You must get to know them better, and they you. You got on famously the other night, but—'

He broke in impatiently, 'Of course I hadn't forgotten the children, Kate. They're all part of us getting to know each other—it couldn't be any other way. Naturally, they're your priority. Believe me, *I know* about children and how much they matter.'

The words, '*I know*', spoken so vehemently, hung in the air. Kate stared up at him. His bright hazel eyes didn't waver. Did he mean what she thought he did? 'Th-that-about children—seemed to come straight from the heart,' she stammered.

'You'd better believe it,' he said dryly. 'I've two of my own.'

He was still holding her shoulders. She shrugged herself away from him. She felt winded, as if she'd been kicked in the stomach. Yet why should she be so shocked? Because he hadn't confided in her sooner, because she had thought him a fancy-free bachelor and felt cheated? 'Why didn't you tell me?' she whispered in a hurt voice.

'I started to once but we were interrupted and there hasn't been another opportunity. I planned to tell you tonight, but. . .' he quirked his mouth into a sardonic half-smile '. . .not quite so abruptly.'

So he had two children. Was he responsible for them? Was he divorced, a widower. . .still married and playing the field, as Paul had done for years? Was it that possibility that so shocked her? Could it possibly be true? Was that why he'd delayed telling her?

A wave of anger washed over her. 'What, when you'd softened me up with food and drink so that I would believe whatever story you choose to give me?' she said in a brittle, bitter voice. She wished the words unsaid as soon as she had uttered them. It was a despicable thing to say — James would never do that. He wasn't Paul.

His usually smiling eyes went cold. He said softly in his deep, grainy voice, 'I don't know what's going through that inventive mind of yours, but I can't believe you mean that, Kate.'

Beyond the hedge several cars swished up the drive in quick succession, as if underlining the fact that hospital life was going on as usual.

The blood came and went on her cheeks. She shook her head slowly. 'No,' she said in a small voice, 'I don't mean that. I'm so sorry, James, it was a dreadful thing to say. Please forgive me.'

His mouth slowly curved into one of his wide, gentle smiles, the bleakness left his eye sand they glowed with their customary warmth.

In a calm, matter-of-fact voice, which she found immensely reassuring, he said, 'Forgive you for blowing your top? Understandable, though you shattered me for a moment. You thought I was keeping you in the dark deliberately to conceal some dark secret, right?'

She nodded.

'Well, I'm not, love. My marriage didn't work out and I was divorced three years ago. By mutual agreement my ex-wife, who has remarried, has custody of the children. But it's all very civilised and I can see them any time, though as they're in the States that isn't as often as I'd like. So you see, I've nothing to hide and I'd no intention of deceiving you.'

He'd spoke very simply as he'd stated his case, not playing for sympathy, which made her reaction even more ridiculous.

She said in a shaky voice, 'I know that, James. I don't know what the hell made me say what I did and jump to conclusions.'

'Old hurts, at a guess,' he said wryly, 'caused by someone who *did* deceive you. But I'm not him. I won't let you down. You can trust me, Katrina, with your children, with your life.' My God, he thought, that sounds pompous but I mean every word of it.

'I do,' she said simply, and stretched up and kissed him on the cheek. She felt suddenly light-hearted, confident, cherished—a mini-disaster had been averted.

His eyes blazed triumphantly for an instant—he had made her happy. 'Good. I'm glad we've got that straight,' he murmured, taking her arm and steering her toward the gate. 'Now, let's continue this conversation over dinner.

I'm absolutely starving. We had a small crisis in the day surgery and I missed out on lunch. We've plenty of food for thought so it's time now to feed the inner man.'

'According to my mother, a sure way to a man's heart,' said Kate, with a chuckle.

'Well, it's one way,' replied James, dropping a kiss on her bent head as she ducked to get into the car.

Kate mulled over the phrase 'food for thought' as they drove out of town towards Greyfriars, the country house hotel where they were to dine. James was right. They had much to think and talk about, so much to find out about each other. She wanted to know *all* about him, but where to begin?

She glanced sideways at him as he concentrated on picking his way through the evening traffic, and he turned his head quickly to flash a smile at her.

Homing in unerringly on her thoughts, he said dryly, 'Go on, love, ask away. I'm all yours.'

'What—now?'

'Why not?'

'I thought you wanted to eat first, talk later.'

'I can cope with a few preliminaries.'

She hesitated for a moment. There was so much she wanted to know. 'Your children—how old are they?'

'Tony's twelve and Sonia ten, barely two years between them.'

'Oh, either side of the twins.'

'Yes, that occurred to me when I had supper with you the other night. Talking to Bess and Philip was a poignant reminder that my two are so far away. I was tempted to say something about having kids of my own just to have an excuse to talk about them.'

His voice was low, husky with suppressed emotion. The

bleakness, the hurt was there in his eyes for a fleeting moment.

If he were a woman, thought Kate, he'd be weeping buckets. She said softly, 'Oh, James, why on earth didn't you?'

'You were uptight about me meeting Bess and Philip, remember? And then so relieved when they had made me welcome and calmly took things in their stride. I was afraid of spoiling the evening because I realised that my news might come as a shock. Thought you'd had enough emotional ups and downs for one day so I decided to wait till tonight to put you in the picture.'

Kate groaned. 'And I nearly messed that up by suspecting the worst. I'm so sorry. I seem to have crossed swords with you since you first arrived at the Memorial. How on earth can you bear with me?'

'Easily,' he said with a soft, throaty laugh as they came to a stop in front of an elegant eighteenth-century mansion. He unfastened his seat belt and then hers, pausing as he leaned across to rub his cheek against her cheek with infinite gentleness. 'Don't ever change, Katrina. I love you just as you are—practical, caring, compassionate, protective, as a mother and a nurse.'

Made speechless and elated by this declaration of love, Kate thrilled to the warmth of his hand at her waist as he guided her up the wide steps into the hotel.

Everything about Greyfriars was gracious. Their table, beside a tall window, overlooked a flagged, balustraded terrace. Great stone urns filled with masses of blood-red trailing geraniums stood at intervals on the balustrade, glowing richly in the westering sunshine.

'It's beautiful,' breathed Kate, when they were seated at the table which was all white damask and gleaming silver. And hideously expensive, she thought, taking one look at the lengthy list of mainly English dishes for which the hotel was famous. She closed the shiny menu with a snap. 'You choose,' she said to James.

'But I don't know your likes and dislikes...yet,' he replied, his hazel eyes twinkling at her intimately over the top of the elegant menu he was studying.

Her heart in her eyes, she smiled back at him. 'I eat anything except veal,' she said.

He ordered watercress soup, smoked trout, lamb cutlets, new potatoes, peas and mangetout, with redcurrant sauce, and fresh strawberry flan and cream to follow.

They drank light, dry, white wine and made small talk while they waited for their food to arrive, but when it did Kate said abruptly what was uppermost in her mind, 'Will you tell me about your marriage, James, and why you got divorced?'

There was a moment's silence and Kate thought he was going to refuse, but with the faintest of smiles he said tersely, 'Tall order, but I'll try. The short answer is that it didn't work from the start and finally ground to a halt. Laura wasn't cut out to be a doctor's wife. I'm not poor, but she's seriously rich and doted on by her father. Loves hunting and the county scene.'

He frowned. 'She hated living in an unfashionable part of London so I could be near the hospital. I worked hard, unsociable hours. *You* would understand, Kate—she didn't. Not that I blame her. I didn't understand her world either. By the time we realised that we had nothing in common, except physical attraction, Tony was a year and a half and Sonia had just been born so we had to make an effort to keep things going for their sakes.'

Kate swallowed the desire to say bitchily, 'Bet you were the one who made all the effort, not the spoilt Laura,' but instead said, 'But you did try to stick together.'

'Oh, we tried, but obviously not hard enough,' James said bitterly, and Kate knew he was blaming himself for not having saved his marriage. 'After a while Laura began taking the children to her father's place in the country for weeks on end. I saw them whenever possible. It was some consolation that the children were young enough to accept my abbreviated visits as the norm so our final separation, when it came, was less traumatic than it might have been.'

But not for you, thought Kate during a pause while their soup plates were replaced by the fish course.

'Did you get divorced so that Laura could marry again?' prompted Kate when the waiter had gone.

'Yes, though, given the state of our marriage, it was inevitable. The advent of Hugo Rothenstein simply precipitated matters.'

'Hugo Rothenstein—sounds like an American.'

'He is, and multi-millionaire-rich. Business associate of Laura's dad. I met him when I was visiting the children. Nice bloke. Ironic isn't it, to like the man who replaces you with your wife? He and Laura are well suited, both horse-mad. But all that matters to me is that Tony and Sonia like him immensely, and as long as they see me from time to time they seem happy enough.'

His eyes sombre, he gave Kate a rueful smile. 'And that,' he added, 'is both a pain and a relief.'

'I can imagine,' murmured Kate, impulsively reaching across the table to touch his hand. 'I'd feel exactly the same about Philip and Bess—glad that they were happy but deep down resenting anyone taking my place with them.'

'That's it exactly.' He grasped her hand and squeezed it. His sombre eyes bean to brighten. 'Of course you understand. We have so much in common, Kate, in both our private and professional lives. The future looks good, my love. We won't let anything spoil it.'

The waiters moved in, and they made nonsense conversation as their fish plates were removed and their lamb cutlets were served.

When the waiters had disappeared James said, 'I'd no idea I'd rambled on for so long—sorry about that.'

Kate shook her head. 'Don't be. I asked you to tell me how your marriage broke up. I *needed* to know, James, to know that you're not. . .' Her voice trailed off.

'That I'm not still in love with Laura?'

'Something like that. It was such a shock, you see, learning that you had been married when I had thought you a fancy-free bachelor.'

'And have I convinced you that I'm not carrying a torch for my ex-wife?' he asked in a dry voice, one quizzical eyebrow raised.

'Oh, yes,' she said breathlessly. 'Absolutely. I shouldn't have doubted you. Thanks for being so frank.'

'I wanted to be, and I hope you'll be just as frank with me, Kate. We must start with a clean slate, clear away the debris of our past mistakes and be totally honest with each other.'

He was right, yet she was reluctant to talk even to James about the utter failure Paul had been as a husband and a father. How could she explain the shame and humiliation she felt at having been deceived by a gambler and a womaniser who couldn't hold down a job and had used her and her parents as a meal ticket?

Kate kept her eyes fixed on her plate and her voice flat. 'There's not much to tell. Paul and I got married when I qualified. We'd planned to start a family straight away, but when I became pregnant he was furious. And when the twins were born he refused to have much to do with them. Then he lost his job and I returned to nursing and he had to look after them while I was at work. Things were a bit difficult.'

Difficult! When he'd neglected the children, began stealing the housekeeping money to finance his gambling... Best not think about that.

She looked up and found James's eyes upon her, warm, compassionate, *knowing*, as if he'd read what was in her mind. She said in a rush, 'It didn't work out. He left home, and we were divorced four years ago. End of story.' There was no way she could say anything more, not now— perhaps one day. Her eyes pleaded with him not to press her.

He didn't, but said very simply, 'I'm sorry you've been so badly hurt, dear love. I'll make it up to you and the children—take care of you all. We'll take things slowly day by day, build a warm, loving relationship—a lasting one. Believe me, I won't let you down.'

'I know you won't,' said Kate, feeling his strength and love reaching out to her, embracing her, protecting her.

They ate the rest of their dinner in an incredibly lighthearted mood. They laughed a lot, jubilant that they had unburdened themselves, and revelled in each other's company, touching hands or feet when they could. They talked of many things, discovering a mutual love of music— classical and jazz—and of the theatre, for Restoration comedy to Ayckbourn, from Shakespeare to Shaw. It was like a good omen, cementing their rapport—their feeling of oneness.

Kate told him about her parents and their nursery, and how marvellous and supportive and loving they were. And James gave her a potted history of his family. His parents, both doctors, lived and worked in India, but were retiring and returning to Scotland in a few months' time. He had a married sister living in New Zealand, and a brother who was a barrister with the Court of Human Rights in The Hague.

'And that's the family, barring an assortment of aunts, uncles and cousins,' he said. 'The Bruce clan are scattered far and wide.'

'Even your own children,' said Kate softly.

'Even my own kids.' A shadow crossed his face for an instant and then was gone, replaced by a tentative, tender smile. 'But I'll be seeing them soon. They're coming over on holiday in August.' He caught her hand across the table and raised it to his lips. 'I'm looking forward to introducing them to you, Katrina—you and the twins.'

For a fleeting moment Kate felt a minuscule flutter of apprehension at the prospect. Just supposing... No, she mustn't even think it. 'It'll be lovely to meet them,' she aid brightly, 'and I'm sure that they and the twins will—'

'Like each other on sight,' James interrupted, with quiet confidence. He lifted his glass and clinked it against hers. 'To us and our precious offspring, Kate, and a future full of promise for all of us.'

His confidence and optimism were reassuring, and Kate said firmly, 'To all of us,' and drained her glass.

An hour later they drove back to town through the moonlit countryside in a warm, thoughtful silence, mute messages of love winging between them.

'Happy?' asked James softly when they drew up in front of the lodge.

Soporific with good food and wine—having drunk most of the wine herself as James was driving—and surprised to find that they had arrived home, Kate murmured sleepily, 'Very. Thank you for making me so happy. I do love you James.' She nuzzled his slightly bristly cheek and said huskily, 'You are coming in for a night cap, aren't you?'

James gave a deep-throated chuckle. 'I think not, love. We're both a bit punch-drunk after this evening, and if I do I won't want to go. And, whatever you think now, you'll hate yourself and me in the morning if I stay. We're embarking on a steady courtship, remember? And first date hopping into bed with one another just isn't on.' He kissed her lightly on her nose and firmly on her lips, and wondered why he was being so noble when what he most wanted to do was to strip off her clothes, and his own, and make passionate love to her.

Hazily, she acknowledged that he was right and, strangely, felt not rejected but cherished. He minded, cared. He escorted her up the garden path, and she allowed him to unlock the door and stand at the bottom of the stairs until she safely reached the top. She turned to look down at him, and he blew her a kiss.

'Sweet dreams, dear heart,' he said softly, as he let himself out and closed the front door behind him.

CHAPTER NINE

FOR Kate, the weeks following the magical evening with James at Greyfriars flew by.

She was busy at home, ferrying the twins to various after-school activities, and at the hospital she was coping with an increased influx of patients due to the expanding local GP practices. But she was in love, and high on adrenalin, and she threw herself joyfully into her work.

The only flaw to her happiness was that she wasn't able to share her happiness with Bess and Philip. Even if she had summoned up the courage, common sense told her that the time was not yet right. It was too soon for them to accept James as more than a casual friend.

But when he began calling in at the lodge occasionally when he was going off duty she thought that they might be curious, giving her an opportunity to hint at something more than friendship, but they never questioned his visits. And they took the news that he was divorced and had a son and daughter of his own just as casually.

Kate had thought this might faze them as it had her, but it did no such thing. They were simply intrigued to learn that Tony and Sonia lived on a stud farm in California, and asked all sorts of probing questions. How old were they? How big was the farm? How many horses were there? Amongst other things, they wanted to know if they ever came to England, and if they did would they get a chance to meet them?

'They'll be coming over in August,' said James, 'and I promise you'll be the first to meet them. In fact, I'm hoping that you'll show them round a bit, perhaps introduce them to some of your friends. They're going to be a bit lost at first, especially when I'm on duty.'

'We'll be only too glad to look after them,' said Bess, sounding very adult, grave and dignified.

And Philip added seriously, 'Don't worry, Dr Bruce, we'll enjoy showing them around. You can depend on us.'

'Thanks, I knew I could,' said James, flashing Kate a triumphant smile. Then he added casually, 'And, now that we're getting to know each other, what about dropping the Dr Bruce and calling me James?'

Their faces lit up. 'Brilliant,' they said in unison.

A truly flaming June turning into a blazing July, bringing hordes of visitors to Millchester. Every day quite a few of them ended up in the already busy minor injuries unit. The staff could normally cope with the steady stream of injuries that arrived on their doorstep, but one brilliantly hot Monday afternoon the stream became a torrent and Colin Peel, the nurse manager, phoned Kate for more help.

'We're packed to the gills,' he said. 'A crowd of youths have just staggered in. They've been having a punch-up, nothing serious—usual cut lips, bloody noses and so on. But they're scaring the other patients so I'd like to get them out as soon as possible.'

'Drunk?'

'Not roaring, but they've had a few.'

'Who's the cas officer on duty?'

'Dr Coggan.' His voice was expressionless.

'Right, leave it with me. I'll have someone with you shortly.'

Mary Coggan, she thought as she put the phone down. A perfectly able GP, but five feet nothing, a bit vague, fiftyish—no physical match for a bunch of rowdy teenagers. Colin and the porter were capable, but would have their hands full. What was needed was a bit more muscle, as well as medical help.

She picked up the phone and bleeped James's number.

He answered immediately. 'Dr Bruce.'

They'd had lunched together only an hour before and his deep, grainy voice was brisk and professional, but it still played havoc with her heart which bumped alarmingly.

'It's Kate,' she announced breathily.

'Kate, how lovely.' His voice dropped a notch, and Kate's toes curled. 'Is this business or pleasure?'

She uncurled her toes and pulled herself together. 'Business, I'm afraid. SOS from Colin Peel. He needs help with a rowdy lot of youths in MIU—'

'I'm on my way.'

'I'll join you there.'

'I'd rather you didn't, Kate.'

Loving him for caring, she said simply, 'It's my job.'

'Then stick with me,' he growled.

'Like a leech,' Kate replied, a smile in her voice.

In MIU, Dr Coggan agreed with James that she and the regular staff would attend to the normal influx of patients whilst he, Kate and Colin took care of the punch-up crowd.

James took one look at the noisy teenagers and insisted that he and Colin worked in adjacent cubicles, with Kate working between the two of them.

'I don't want you alone with any of these young thugs,' he said.

Kate protested, but was overruled by both men.

'It makes sense,' said Colin bluntly. 'We're not talking male chauvinism here—just brute strength if it's necessary. We've got it, you haven't. It's what you would advise for any other female nurse in the circumstances, Kate.'

He was dead right and she gave it without further argument.

While the three of them treated the sometimes abusive young men in the cubicles Vic, the tough middle-aged porter, kept those waiting for treatment segregated in a corner of Reception, away from the other patients waiting to be seen by Dr Coggan.

For an hour they worked flat out until only three subdued lads were waiting for attention and something like peace reigned. But as James was stitching together a badly mauled and bitten ear and Kate was at the other side of the couch giving an anti tetanus injection there was a commotion in Reception, and Vic shouted, 'Can someone come? One of them's passed out.'

Colin called from the next cubicle, 'I can't go—I'm in the middle of stitching.'

'Snap,' James muttered.

Kate said. 'I'll go. I've finished here.'

She swished out through the curtains before James could object, and hurried across to where Vic and two of the youths were grouped round the collapsed figure of the third, who was lying huddled on the floor.

'He just sort of doubled up and groaned and slid off the chair,' said Vic.

Kate knelt down beside the prostrate body. The youth was lying half on his side, his knees drawn up to his abdomen. His face was waxen pale, filmy with sweat and screwed up with pain, but he wasn't unconscious. He was eighteen and his name was Ray Bennet, Kate learned from his mates.

'It's me stomach,' he gasped, as Kate bent over him. 'Came on sudden. Sods kicked me or summink.'

'Fetch a wheelchair, Vic, and we'll get him into a cubicle,' said Kate briskly, taking the lad's pulse as she spoke. Fast, weak, thready...an internal injury, rupture, haemorrhage? She didn't like his colour or the way he was breathing. She would give him a whiff of oxygen while she was waiting for James to take a look at him.

A few minutes later, having first examined Ray's chest, James looked grim as he pressed his fingers lightly over the lad's skinny flat abdomen and listened through his stethoscope for bowel sounds. From his ribs to his pelvis Ray was a mass of angry red welts and contusions, some of which were already beginning to turn purple. Gentle as James was, the young man yelped and gasped with pain when James touched a spot midline, just below the ribs.

'Sorry about that, Ray,' said James. 'I'm going to take your blood pressure, and then give you something for the pain.' His face was expressionless when he took the BP reading. He nodded to Kate. 'Five milligrams of morphine, please, Sister.'

At that moment Colin popped his head round the curtain. 'Anything I can do?' he asked.

'Arrange an ambulance for the uni—intensive care, abdominal emergency, may need vascular intervention,' James replied softly.

While Kate drew up the injection and gave it he told Ray that he was to be transferred to the university hospital in Porthampton for observation. He went on to explain, 'You may be bleeding inside, and they've got experts who can deal with that so the sooner we get you there the better. Don't worry, you'll be in good hands.'

The morphine had begun to work, and Ray mumbled drowsily, 'Whatever you say, Doc, just as long as they get rid of this pain.'

'That'll be their number one priority,' replied James reassuringly, but his eyes, when they met Kate's across the recumbent figure, were bleak.

They put up the side rails and moved to the end of the couch.

'He's in a bad way, isn't he?' whispered Kate.

James nodded. 'His BP's pretty low. I'd rather not have given him an analgesic till he's been fully examined—don't like masking the symptoms. But the pain's contributing to the shock as much as the bleed, and we need to keep him quiet and rested. I think the aorta may be under pressure, and if that should rupture...' His voice trailed off.

'He's in real trouble,' murmured Kate, thinking of the massive bleed that could result from damage to the main blood vessel to the heart.

The ambulance arrived a few minutes later and Ray Bennet was dispatched in the care of two experienced paramedics to the teaching hospital in Porthampton.

'It's damned frustrating,' muttered James savagely after they'd seen their patient off, 'not to be able to do more. Having to send him off to be investigated elsewhere. With a fully operational theatre we could have done a laparotomy ourselves and got things sorted out.'

Kate looked up into his angry face and felt suddenly apprehensive. Was he already regretting working in a small provincial hospital—longing for the opportunity to use his talents in a teaching hospital? He'd seemed so happy, but...

'Are you sorry you came to the Memorial, James?' she asked, a slight tremble in her voice. 'Would you rather be somewhere doing major surgery?'

James came to an abrupt halt in the doorway of the duty office. Astonishment replaced the anger in his face and he took her roughly by the arm and pushed her into the empty room, snapping the door shut behind him with his foot.

He turned her to face him and pulled her into his arms.

'Sorry I came to the Memorial—are you *mad*? Of course I'm not sorry. I regret not being able to follow through a case like this, but I'm a physician as well as a surgeon and here I can practise both disciplines. And, as if that were not enough, I've got you.' He planted a hard, painful kiss on her mouth. 'There, does that satisfy you?'

'Oh, yes, absolutely,' she said, taken aback by his tone and the savage kiss.

'Then stop doubting me, Kate,' he ground out, and released her abruptly, then opened the door and strode out of the room.

Kate took a deep breath and followed him moments later, hoping to find him and tell him that she didn't doubt him. But he'd already left the unit and, after completing forms relating to the afternoon's activities, so did she.

He phoned that evening when she was preparing supper and said, without preamble, 'Kate, take Wednesday off. I've arranged cover—you do the same. We both need time to be alone together—no children, no hospital. We'll have coffee at my place—I want to show you around—and then out somewhere for a pub lunch.'

'But—'

'No buts, Kate, do it...for us.'

Her heart bounded against her ribs. He asked so little of her. He'd been patient and loving, and to spend the day with him would be heaven. There was no reason why she shouldn't. There was full cover on all the wards and departments and Maggie would be in the office.

'I'd love to,' she said breathlessly, refusing to worry about how the twins would take it.

They took it as casually as they seemed to take most things these days.

'Fancy you and James bunking off,' said Philip with a grin.

And Bess said, in her recently acquired adult manner, 'Hope you have a brilliant day, Mum. You both work so jolly hard—you deserve it.'

James, wearing pale moleskin trousers over muscular thighs and a check shirt open at the neck, revealing the strong column of his throat, arrived at nine-thirty on Wednesday. The sun glinted on his thick, dark brown hair. He looked muscular, healthy, craggily handsome.

Again Kate was waiting for him in the garden, as she had that evening weeks before, and again, almost hidden by the hedge, he kissed her in spite of the drive being busy with passing cars. But this time she didn't protest. She kissed him back firmly, eagerly. She didn't care that if they were seen the grapevine, which had been humming gently over the last few weeks, would be buzzing by the evening.

'You look like one of those strong, incredibly handsome lumberjacks in an advertisement,' she said with a little chuckle as he crushed her against him.

'And you look like a wood nymph in his pale honey-brown frock and with your hair all burnished and shimmering,' he said. He fingered the bootlace straps and brushed his lips across her bare, tanned shoulder. 'It's hard to tell where *you* end and the dress begins,' he murmured. 'You're a bewitching witch of a woman, Kate, and I love you.'

Kate shivered and nuzzled the triangle of dark curly hair at his throat. She felt light-headed, free of all inhibitions. She said huskily, 'And I want to make love to you, James, mad, sexy, passionate love.'

His arms tightened round her waist. 'Is that a promise,

Katrina Brown?' he asked lightly, but his hazel eyes were serious as they stared into hers.

'Yes,' she said simply, her voice low and firm. There was no doubt in her now. She loved this man and she wanted him.

His breathing quickened and his eyes blazed with sudden desire, matching the yearning in her own. He said thickly, 'In that case, my darling, what are we standing here for? Let's go.'

They drove in silence, their urgent need to make love vibrating between them, electric, magnetic.

After what seemed an endless journey, though it was only a few miles along the coast, they pulled up in front of a long, low, two-storey building, topped with a miniature glass cupola. It was all pristine white stucco, with large windows and little balconies looking south across the channel.

But it barely registered with Kate as she stepped out of the car. Without a word, James took her by the hand and led her quickly through the front door, across a black and white tiled hall, of which she was hazily aware, up a curved staircase and into a lofty bedroom that opened off a wide landing.

For an instant Kate hung back in the doorway to stare in amazement at the large four-poster, covered in rich, red damask, that dominated the room.

'Venetian. Inherited with the house from my eccentric great-uncle,' murmured James, drawing her toward the bed.

'It's beautiful,' breathed Kate.

'*You're* beautiful,' grated James, taking her roughly into his arms in a bone-crushing hug. 'And I want you, Katrina. God, how I want you.' She could feel him hard and rigid with need as he ran his hands down her back, cupped her bottom and pressed her even closer.

'And I want you,' she sighed as she strained against him, feeling her nipples peak with longing, her own arousal soft and moist between her thighs.

And suddenly they were kissing—breathing hard—tugging at each other's clothes. His fingers unzipped her dress, slid the straps off her shoulders and unfastened her bra, while hers unbuttoned his shirt, fumbled at his trousers and his underpants. And then they were naked, except for the minuscule barrier of Kate's lacy panties.

James slid them down over her slender hips, laid her down on the bed and kissed her dark bushy triangle. She gasped with pleasure, arched to meet his lips and tongue and whispered, 'Oh, James.' She ran her fingers through his hair.

He lifted his head sharply, and muttered hoarsely, 'Wait—must get something—won't be a moment.'

Kate held her breath and closed her eyes and heard him scrabbling in the small chest beside the bed. He swore savagely, and she opened her eyes and said softly, 'Here, let me.' Taking the condom from his usually competent fingers, she fitted it tenderly, gently, over his strong, proud erection.

They made wild, uninhibited love quickly in an explosion of passion that neither could contain—kissing, nuzzling, biting, sucking, until Kate's breasts felt as if they would burst with longing and James was hard and pulsing rhythmically deep inside her—until they peaked together in a long, shuddering orgasm, leaving them sweaty and breathless.

'Sorry, my darling, I couldn't make it last. I just couldn't wait,' panted James ruefully, kissing her salty lips and taking her with him as he rolled on his side. 'Do better next time.'

'It was fantastic,' murmured Kate, returning his kiss. 'I couldn't wait either.' She raised herself on an elbow and smiled down at him. 'Is there going to be a next time?' she asked demurely.

He grinned, and his hazel eyes danced. 'More than one next time,' he said drowsily. 'We've got all day.'

Kate sighed happily as she laid her head down on the pillow beside him. 'Mmm, lovely,' she murmured as sleep claimed her.

They had been sleeping for what seemed minutes but, in fact, turned out to have been over two hours when the phone rang.

'Thought you weren't on call,' mumbled Kate.

'I'm not,' said James, nuzzling her cheek as he turned away to pick up one of the two handsets on the bedside chest. 'This is my personal mobile so it's family or friends. Don't worry, I'll be brief—nothing's going to spoil our day.'

But Kate didn't need second sight to know that this wasn't true when he sat bolt upright a moment later and said in a surprised voice, 'Laura!' He went on fearfully, 'The children—are they all right?' A moment later he said, 'Thank God!' A wave of relief passed over his face, and Kate felt her own stomach muscles, which had knotted up at the fear in his voice, unclench.

'I'll go,' she whispered, sitting up

He shook his head and took her hand. 'Stay,' he mouthed back.

So she stayed and held his hand and listened to the one-sided conversation, catching an occasional word, like 'accident' and 'traumatised' which made her stomach knot up again, until at last the call came to an end.

James put the mobile down and said in a shocked

staccato voice, 'Poor old Hugo's had a riding accident a bad one—spinal injuries, complete paraplegia. He's been taken to a special clinic. It'll be a long job. Laura wants me to have the children so she can stay with him indefinitely. And, apparently, the kids have asked to come to me. They're pretty distressed—they were with Hugo when it happened.'

Kate said softly, 'Oh, James, how dreadful for them. No wonder they want to be with you if they can't be with their mother.' She kissed him gently on the cheek. 'They're going to need you. Do you know when they're coming?'

'They're coming the day after tomorrow.' His troubled eyes brightened. He gave her a hug and a fierce, hard kiss. 'Kate, Tony and Sonia will be here the day after tomorrow—I can't believe it. I'm damned sorry it's happened for the reason that it has but I'll be so glad to have my children with me—be around because they need me. Do I sound unspeakably selfish, Kate?'

She shook her head. 'No, you sound like a caring, loving father,' she said firmly.

'They're coming the day after tomorrow!'

Lying in bed that night and reviewing the day's events, Kate repeated James's words out loud. Resolutely she refused to let herself think of the earlier part of the day, which had begun so joyfully with their wild, uninhibited lovemaking and had ended so shatteringly with the news from across the Atlantic.

By mutual, unspoken consent they hadn't made love again but had held each other tenderly for a while, like lovers familiar with waking in each other's arms. And they'd showered and dressed with the same familiar intimacy, not talking much.

Then James had led her down the elegant curving staircase, across the black and white hall to a large, gleaming kitchen, and there they had talked, frankly and at length, over bread and cheese and wine about how they should deal with the new situation confronting them.

They had no illusions about how deeply this would effect their immediate future, and possibly their long-term one.

From the day after tomorrow there would be two sets of children to cope with. No longer would James be separated from Tony and Sonia by several thousand miles, reassured that they were happy with their mother and stepfather and on a daily basis largely unaffected by his developing relationship with Kate.

Suddenly the situation had been stood on its head and *his* children, rather than Bess and Philip, would be the most vulnerable and, for a while at least, would need his undivided love and attention.

As they were finishing their lunch James touched his glass to hers and said quietly, 'I'm afraid we'll have to put everything on hold for a bit, Kate, which is ironic, considering that we were about to come clean with the twins. But I shall have to introduce you to my two just as a friend. They won't be able to cope with anything more at present.'

Even though she knew that this was inevitable for one appalling moment she found herself resenting his children, innocent as they were. Why did they have to come on the scene now, just when everything was coming right for her and James?

Horrified by such a shameful thought, she squashed it savagely and her true, caring, compassionate nature quickly reasserted itself. But she was shaken to the core by her reaction, and said passionately, to reassure herself as much as him, 'Of *course* they must come first, no question of that. And however you want to play this is all right by me.'

She leaned over and kissed him hard on the mouth, and said softly, 'You told me once to trust myself and my children to you, James. Now I'm telling you that you can put your trust in me to do whatever is right for you and *your* children, even if it does mean keeping our love under wraps for a while yet. I'm prepared to go at whatever pace you set.'

And James smiled into her eyes, took her hands into his, gently kissed the palms and said simply, 'My life's in your hands, Katrina.'

It might have sounded sentimental and sloppy but it didn't. It was just a matter-of-fact statement, confirming his love for her, and there was nothing more to say on the matter. And she, suppressing her hammering heartbeats and a desire to throw herself into his arms, became brisk and practical.

Who would look after Tony and Sonia when he was on duty, and who would he ask to cover him at the hospital over the next week while he took time off to settle them in?

He teased her gently for being bossy. He was sure that Mrs Bee, his treasure of a housekeeper whom he's inherited with the house and who lived in the studio flat over the garage, would be in her element, caring for the children.

And to locum for him, semi-retired Jim Pierce would probably jump at the chance. James would phone him immediately to find out if he was free. He was, and readily agreed to cover from Friday.

So everything that can be done to prepare for the arrival of James's children has been done, thought Kate, punching her pillow angrily and willing sleep to come. But, whispered a small voice as at last her eyelids began to drop, are you prep—? And then she slipped into blessed oblivion and slept soundly till morning.

CHAPTER TEN

KATE had snatched glimpses of James on Thursday. He was operating from early morning to late evening. Everyone was working flat out to reduce the elective surgery lists before the August holiday season began in earnest.

She had a few moments' conversation with him when she was helping out in the surgical ward. She was settling the most recent patient back from the recovery unit when James popped in to check on the post-op cases.

'How are they all doing?' he asked softly, suddenly appearing at the opposite side of the bed.

He was in his surgical greens, His cap was pushed back from his forehead, which glistened with sweat, and a mask dangled round his neck. It was late afternoon. He looked tired, drawn. Deep lines scored down his cheeks and his usually dancing eyes were anxious.

It's not operating that's bothering him, thought Kate. He takes that in his stride. He's worried sick about his children, and so would I be if it were the twins in the same situation.

She said in a low voice, 'They're all doing fine. Their obs are good—no one to worry about. What's more to the point, how are you, love?'

'Working an auto,' he said laconically. 'Finding it bloody hard to concentrate, terrified of falling down on the job.'

'Well, you haven't, as I said. Everyone's fine—come and see for yourself.'

They moved from bed to bed. Recent post-op patients

were peacefully sleeping off their anaesthetics, and patients who had been operated on earlier in the day were propped up and taking notice. James spoke to them in his usual easy fashion, asking how they were feeling. Most complained of feeling sore, but were reassured that this was normal and would wear off in time. A couple were amazingly bright and were raring to get up and about.

'You see,' said Kate, as she accompanied him to the ward door, 'no disasters. You're as on the ball as ever.'

He raised a smile. 'I do seem to have taken out all the right bits,' he said, 'but, oh, Kate, I'll be damned glad to get tomorrow over and have my kids where safe and sound—see how they are for myself.'

She squeezed his hand. 'It won't be long now, my darling. 'I'll be thinking of you. Promise you'll ring me when you get back from Gatwick, however late.'

'Promise,' he said. He brushed his lips across her cheek, turned on his heel and walked brisky down the corridor towards the theatre suite.

He phoned late on Friday evening when Kate had nearly given him up. 'The plane was delayed,' he explained.

'How are the children?'

'Completely jet-lagged. They've not said much, though they seem very happy to be with me. They've crashed out and I hope that after a good sleep they'll open up and talk about what's happened. I don't want to pressurise them but just reassure them that I'm their dad, and here when they need me.' He sounded infinitely sad and weary.

Kate said softly, 'I'm sure they know that, my love. That's why they wanted to come to you. Things will look better in the morning. Right now you need your bed, too.' She wished she could hold him in her arms, feel his strong arms about her, feel their bodies clamped together in a hot, sweaty orgasm of love. Her pulses raced at the thought of it.

He must have read her thoughts. 'I just wish you were in it.' His voice was a gruff baritone. 'I could do with a hug and much more beside.'

'So could I,' she murmured breathlessly.

He gave a bark of sardonic laughter, and said wryly, 'Fat chance of that. When the time is right to get the children together we'll have four pairs of critical eyes upon us.'

Surprised by his almost defeatist tone, which was so unlike him, Kate said crisply, 'Oh, come on, James, don't be so pessimistic. They may not be critical. And as for getting them together, the sooner the better. Why not tomorrow afternoon? Suggest it to Tony and Sonia. It may be just what they need—to meet other people and be welcomed by kids of their own age.'

'You know, Kate, you could be right. I'm being over-protective, aren't I, assuming they want me exclusively? What rubbish. They're normal, gregarious, happy children like Bess and Philip, and I'm treating them like fragile invalids. You're dead right, love. The sooner our two broods get together the better.'

Kate heaved a sigh of relief. He was back to normal. 'Good, then, that's settled. Now, please, darling, go to bed and have a good night's sleep. You've had a hell of a few days.'

'Made bearable by you.'

Her heartbeat quickened. 'Flatterer. Goodnight, James.'

'Goodnight, Katrina.'

Over breakfast on Saturday morning Kate announced that James would probably be bringing Tony and Sonia over to meet them that afternoon.

'Oh, brill,' said her offspring predictably.

'But you may find them a bit subdued,' Kate warned. 'James said that they're pretty jet-lagged after travelling six thousand miles.'

Bess looked thoughtful. 'And they must be utterly shattered of what's happened to their stepfather,' she said. 'James was telling us the other day that he's a really fab sort of person, and they like him a lot. Though, of course,' she added, 'they've got their real dad, and he's fab, too.'

'That's true,' Philip agreed, 'but their stepfather's a nice enough guy, and it must have been pretty grim for them, being with him when he had his accident and nearly died. Do you think we should say anything about it, Mum?'

'I think we should play it by ear,' said Kate, quietly rejoicing at their remarks about James. 'They may not want to talk about it. Leave it to them unless an opportunity to say something crops up naturally. Otherwise, just make them feel welcome.'

'Natch!' said Philip, at his most laconic.

'I wonder what they look like?' mused Bess.

Kate recalled seeing a silver-framed photograph of the children on the chest beside the canopied bed where she and James had made love. She had meant to ask about it, but. . . She blushed at the memory and busied herself clearing the dishes.

'We'll just have to wait and see,' she said, hoping she sounded calmer then she felt at the prospect of meeting them.

The rest of the morning was spent in a frenzy of activity. She baked cakes and chivvied the twins into cleaning the garden furniture and setting it out on the little brick patio. The brightly striped umbrella, competing with the flower-beds, made it look rather continental.

'We'll have drinks out here,' she said briskly. 'Make them feel at home...you know, barbecues, space and things.' She waved her hand round the acre of garden.

Philip hooted with laughter. 'Come on, Mum, where's your usual cool? What's with this red-carpet treatment—who're you trying to impress? They're not American, and not royalty either—they're just James's kids.'

Just James's kids, thought Kate. If you did but know, son, they're much more important than royalty to me, to us.

She shrugged and smiled. 'You're dead right,' she said. 'I have been flapping. I just want to...' She trailed off. It was impossible to explain why they were so special, without giving herself away.

Bess said seriously, 'What you mean, Mum, is because they've had a shock and are a long way from home you want to give them a bit of TLC to make up for it.'

Kate heaved a sigh of relief. 'That's it exactly,' she said, and wondered, not for the first time, at her daughter's perceptiveness and ability to get to the heart of a matter.

It was mid-afternoon when James and the children arrived.

Kate's heart turned over when she saw them—James's children. Please let them like us, she prayed.

Tony was tall for his age, a younger version of James, boyishly thin though already showing promise of his father's broad-shouldered physique. And he had the same dark brown hair, cropped very short into almost a crew cut, and the same hazel eyes.

Sonia was plumpish, had large, almond-shaped, green-grey eyes, a cloud of reddish-gold curly hair, a wide, generous mouth inherited from James and dimples.

There was a flurry of slightly self-conscious handshakes when James introduced them. They said, 'How do you do?' rather formally to Kate, and 'Hi,' rather cautiously to Bess and Philip.

Then Bess said to Sonia in her direct fashion, 'Wow, fab hair, utterly brilliant—wish mine was like that.'

Sonia beamed at her. 'I was just wishing that I had hair like yours. It's like silver-gold, and so long—wow.' She reached over Bess's shoulder and tugged at her thick plait of sun-bleached hair.

Bess said dramatically, 'Ouch!' Then she laughed.

It was like a trigger, and suddenly the awkwardness was gone and everyone was laughing and talking.

Kate heaved a sigh of relief. It was going to be all right. To keep the party atmosphere going, working on the premise that growing lads could eat any time, she waved a hand towards the laden table, and said, 'Don't stand on ceremony. Help yourselves to food and drink whenever you're ready.'

Like locusts, the children descended on the goodies. They piled their plates with sandwiches and cakes, armed themselves with cans of Coke and drifted off down the garden to sit on the grass beneath the medlar tree.

They left James and Kate, sitting side by side, at the table.

James said in a dry voice, 'Well, I'm damned. I think we've been dumped.' His eyes twinkled. 'And to think I was worried stiff about them meeting each other.'

'So was I,' said Kate, and told him how Philip had teased her about fussing and how Bess had seemed to understand.

Beneath the shelter of the table James took her hand and massaged her wrist sensuously with his thumb. She trembled. He smiled and said softly, 'She's a remarkable girl, Kate. Very perceptive. She started the ball rolling just now by generously admiring Sonia's hair.'

'And Sonia did her bit,' Kate replied, 'returning the compliment.'

'Yes. It's quite true. Girls are much better communicators than boys, though our two don't seem to be having any problems right now.' He glanced down the garden to where the four children were deep in animated conversation, totally absorbed in each other.

Following his gaze, Kate said, 'Tony and Sonia aren't as subdued as I expected them to be. You were so worried about them last night.'

'I was, but I'd forgotten how resilient children can be. Fourteen hours' sleep and a huge breakfast, and they're almost back to normal. And they phoned Laura just before we left, and she was happier about Hugo. The results of some of the tests he's had look more hopeful and, given time, he may make a better recovery than at first thought.'

'Oh, that's wonderful. No wonder they're happy.'

'Yes, and I'm happy because they are and because it means that I'm going to have them with me for a while, not just have them for flying visits.' He turned to look at her, his eyes serious. 'Knowing that it will put a hold on things for us, does it surprise you, Kate, that I should feel this way?'

Kate shook her head. '*No*,' she said emphatically. 'As I said before, it means that you are a loving father, which is as it should be. I wouldn't have it any other way. As for us, we've got enough love for each other and our children, and I can't explain it but I've got a good feeling about things.'

'And who am I to argue with that?' said James. Seeing that their offspring weren't paying them any attention, he raised her hand to his lips and kissed her fingertips, adding, in his deepest, grainiest voice, 'I love you, my darling Katrina.'

The good feeling remained with her for the rest of the afternoon and evening, when they played noisy card games and ate supper in the kitchen. It was as if they had known each other for years, she thought with quiet satisfaction, looking round at their happy, smiling faces. She caught James's eye, and saw that he was thinking the same thing.

'Happy families,' he whispered, under cover of the shouts of laughter going on around them.

At the end of the evening, when they were saying their goodbyes and regretting that they had to part, he suggested that they all lunched together the following day.

'We'll go to Admiral's Point,' he said. 'That's a locally famous pub restaurant overlooking the harbour in Porthampton,' he explained to Tony and Sonia. 'You'll like it, plenty going one—Shipping in the harbour, liners, naval craft, private yachts. And there's an old-fashioned arcade on the pier—we could visit that. How does that grab you?'

The children were all for it, and so was Kate. It meant another day in his company and a chance for the young people to further their friendship.

She smiled at James, and their eyes locked for an instant. 'It's a lovely idea,' she murmured breathlessly. 'Let's hope the weather holds.'

'Oh, it will,' said James confidently.

He was right. Sunday was a bright but breezy day, with banks of clouds scudding across the blue skies. It was perfect for their outing. The harbour would be at its best.

James, Tony and Sonia arrived, not in the elderly Rover but in a brand new, sleek, six-seater, state-of-the-art space van.

Philip and Bess said, 'Wow, brilliant.' They went to admire the shiny maroon paintwork.

Kate just stared for a moment, and then said to James, 'I thought we'd have to use two cars. How did you manage this?'

'Bit of forward planning. Took delivery last week. Ordered it when I knew that Tony and Sonia would be coming in August. Thought that we might do some touring around. But today seemed an ideal opportunity to christen it.' He quirked a secret smile at her. 'Just right for a family of six,' he said.

It was a tender, intimate moment to cherish, thought Kate as they drove into Porthampton.

After a magnificent lunch at Admiral's Point and a trip over wind-ruffled seas round the harbour they visited the Victorian pier. They played the ancient slot machines, and fell about laughing at the simple entertainment provided by the hall of distorting mirrors.

'Now, what about a cream tea?' said James, as they left the pier and walked along the busy promenade to where he'd parked the car. 'Any suggestions, anybody? Preferably something olde worlde and full of rustic charm.'

'The Thatched Barn,' sang out Philip and Bess in unison.

'Like the sound of it,' said James.

Kate said, 'Oh, I'm not sure. . .' She stopped.

The children forged ahead.

'Why not?' asked James, taking her arm and steering her round a group of teenagers playing a ghetto-blaster.

She said hesitantly, 'It's my parents' place.'

'But I thought they ran a nursery garden centre.'

'They do. The barn is part of the nursery, and in summer they do cream teas with their own strawberries and other soft fruit.'

'Sounds delightful.' He squeezed her arm and she felt the familiar tingle where his fingers rested. 'It's time I met them, Kate—' he was serious '—even if it's just as a friend and colleague.'

'They know that you're that. I've mentioned you and so have the twins, but my mother will take one look at us together and know how we feel about each other.'

'Does that matter? She's not going to blurt it out to the kids, is she?'

'Of course not.'

'Is she going to resent me stealing her daughter's heart?'

'Quite the opposite. She's been hoping that I'd meet someone ever since—'

'Paul walked out on you?'

Kate nodded.

'Then let's round off this extraordinarily happy weekend in style, and let your parents inspect their future—even if they don't officially know it—son-in-law.' He smiled down at her, his eyes twinkling yet full of tenderness.

She stopped walking abruptly, drew in a deep breath and looked sideways up at him. 'Is that a proposal, Dr Bruce?' she asked in a slightly wobbly voice.

'It is. We've spoken of love and our future and our children's future, but not formally of marriage. It's not possible yet but it will be one day, sooner rather than later, I hope.' He turned her to face him squarely. 'So, will you marry me, Katrina, when the time is right?'

'*When* the time is right,' she breathed, 'I will.' Taking advantage of the anonymity of the crowded promenade and the fact that the children were well ahead, she stood on tiptoe and kissed him soundly on his wide, generous mouth.

Quietly elated, with hands almost touching, they walked

back to the car where the four young people were waiting patiently.

Half an hour's drive out of Porthampton took them to West Millchester Sands and the nursery lying just off the coast road.

They approached the cluster of half-timbered and thatched buildings via a drive fringed with ornamental trees and shrubs and roses. Through the trees could be glimpsed greenhouses, glinting in the sunshine, and on rising ground beyond they could see beds of strawberries and neat rows of raspberry canes.

The nursery was busy, the car park nearly full.

'We'll park in front of the cottage,' said Kate, 'though Mum and Dad won't be there. They'll be in the garden shop or the greenhouses.' She directed James down a short curving drive, marked PRIVATE, leading off the main concourse.

The cottage, hidden in a nest of trees and bushes, was low and rambling and, like the other buildings, half-timbered and thatched. Dark red roses rambled up to the thatched roof.

'Idyllic,' said James, breathing in the scent of the roses as he stood beside Kate on the drive.

The children piled noisily out of the car.

'Mum, we'll go and find Gran and Grandpa, and let them know we're here,' said Philip, ushering the others along the drive.

'They'll be busy. Tell them that we'll meet them in the barn for tea when they're free—there's no hurry,' called Kate, as they disappeared round the bushes.

James put his arm round her waist and hugged her to his side.

'Nervous, love? Putting off the moment—afraid I won't

pass muster?' he teased gently. He kissed the top of her head. 'Oh, ye of little faith. What's happened to the good feeling you have about us? It's been vindicated so far—everything's worked like a dream. The children have taken to each other like the proverbial ducks to water, and I've got a feeling that your parents and I are going to do likewise.'

And they did, from the word go.

The children, stuffed full with wholemeal scones and jam and strawberries and cream, had already left the table when Kate's parents joined her and James in the barn.

Kate introduced them rather stiffly. 'Mum, Dad, this is James, James Bruce. James, my parents—Bill and Jessie Orwell.'

James, standing up to shake hands, apologised for the children's absence. 'My two are hell-bent on exploring, and Philip and Bess are only too eager to act as guides,' he explained. 'They assured me that they have your permission to wander around. I hope they won't get in anyone's way.'

'They won't,' said Bill. 'The twins will see to that. They know all the dos and don'ts—they spend a lot of time here.'

'Tony and Sonia will be fine,' Jessie confirmed firmly. 'They seem to be getting on well with our grandchildren, though I gather they only met yesterday. We had quite a long chat. They said something about an accident...their stepfather. Apparently he's been badly injured?' She looked a question at James.

Bill said gruffly, 'You're probing, Jess,' he added to James, with a wink, 'Failing of the women in this family—they're curious and they're bossy.'

Eyes gleaming, James glanced sideways at Kate. 'So

I've noticed,' he said dryly, and added, 'But it's no secret about Hugo—he was thrown from a horse. I'm glad the children mentioned it. They were with him when it happened. It was traumatic for them and I feel they need to talk about it, though they've said very little to me.'

'Perhaps they found it easier to talk to a comfortable granny figure,' said Jessie.

Kate let the conversation flow round her, contributing occasionally as she watched their faces, all dear and familiar to her. They talked with the enthusiasm of people who had discovered an instinctive liking for each other, and there were no embarrassing pauses. It was a repeat of the evening when James had first met Bess and Philip, she thought. The same atmosphere of mutual regard was there.

They exchanged views on many things, but inevitably they ended up talking shop. Plants and nurture, patients and treatment. James was fascinated by the similarities in their fields of work, what with blood analysis, soil analysis, acid and alkaline tests and suchlike.

It was new to him. He was eager to find out more. 'Do you think I might have a look round?' he asked.

Kate could have hugged him. It would please her father no end, though it wasn't, she knew, said for effect. He was genuinely interested.

'Thought you'd never ask,' said Bill, a huge grin on his handsome, rather cherubic face which glowed with health beneath a thatch of silvery-grey hair. He stood up. 'Will you come?' he asked Jess and Kate.

They looked at each other.

'No,' said Jess, 'we've a lot to talk about.'

I'm about to get the third degree, thought Kate as she watched James and her father, both large men, stride shoulder to shoulder out of the room. But she didn't really mind. It might be weeks, months even before she and James could confide in their children, but there was no reason why they shouldn't take her parents into their confidence. It would be a relief to talk.

Jessie was smiling at her. 'He's special, Kate, isn't he?' she said softly, touching Kate's hand.

Kate nodded. 'We only met in May, but I feel I've known him for ever. Does that sound weird?'

Jessie shook her head. 'No,' she said emphatically, 'it sounds like love. It's the way it happened with your father and me.'

'James proposed this afternoon.'

'And. . .?'

'I said yes.'

'Oh, darling, I am pleased. Of course, we know little about him, except that he's divorced and his wife and children live in America, but I certainly like what I've seen. He's obviously a dedicated doctor with a nice sense of humour—very important, that.' She stood up, her still-pretty faced wreathed in smiles. 'This calls for some bubbly. Let's go to the cottage and break out a bottle.'

As they walked to the cottage Kate said dryly, 'I won't say no to a drink, but it's too soon to celebrate. We haven't told the children yet. As far as they're concerned, we're just friends—nothing more. And that's the way it's got to stay for a while until they're good and ready to accept the situation.'

Jessie looked surprised. 'I assumed they knew. Pity you have to wait to tell them,' she said. 'It's so obvious that they like and admire James. They're always full of him when they come to visit. I should have thought that they would be delighted by the news.'

'Oh, Mum, do you really think so?'

'Yes.' Jessie nodded.

Kate took a deep breath. 'I'm glad you think that. But even if it's true it doesn't alter things. We haven't only Bess and Philip to think about now—there's Tony and Sonia. They've had enough shocks recently—they're not ready to take any more changes on board. We've got to give them time to get to know me.' She gave Jessie a hug. 'But I'm so glad that you and Dad know about James and me.'

Her mother hugged her back. 'Life's a bitter-sweet time for you at the moment, love,' she said gently, 'but everything will fall into place eventually. I have a feeling in my bones, as my mother used to say. But someday soon you'll have to take the plunge and tell the children. They're all bright and, however circumspect you are, you won't be able to keep them in the dark too long.'

She paused, and swallowed a mouthful of gin and tonic. 'Don't underestimate them, Kate. They may understand more than you think. Give them a chance to be generous.'

Kate would have liked to pursue this enigmatic statement further, but at that moment the others returned and the conversation became noisy and general.

Bill and Jessie wanted them to stay for supper, but James explained that they were waiting for a phone call that evening, giving the latest bulletin on Hugo, so they stayed only long enough to have a quick drink—whiskey for Bill, mineral water for James, and lemonade and biscuits for the children, whose appetites seemed bottomless.

Not, thought Kate, the celebratory drink that her mother had wanted but, nevertheless, a happy end to a happy day. She glanced round at everyone and found James's eyes upon her, tender and warmly amused. He smiled and raised his glass in silent salute from across the room, then touched it to his lips and drank and she felt, even at that distance, wrapped around by his love and was elated by their own, private celebration.

Kate mulled over her mother's words as they were driving back to the lodge a little later. Was she right? Should they take the plunge soon and let the children in on their secret? Would they understand? They'd got off to a marvellous start. They all seemed so easy with each other and had already established a rapport. Nothing must be allowed to spoil that, she thought fiercely, however difficult it was for her and James to maintain this façade of friendship.

She clenched her fists in her lap. James took a hand off the steering-wheel and covered them briefly.

'Don't worry, it'll all come right,' he murmured, under cover of the children's chatter.

Kate unclenched her hands and giggled. 'Do you feel it in your bones, too?'

James pulled a face. 'Sorry, love, the allusion escapes me,' he said.

'That's what my mother said—that she felt in her bones that everything would come right for us. The omens are good.'

He chuckled. 'Smart lady. So she knows all, and approves?' He sounded pleased.

'Yes.'

'I'm glad. I think your father feels the same.'

Kate was incredulous. 'You told him about us?'

'We didn't have a heart-to-heart, like you probably had with your mother, but we understood each other by a kind of osmosis. We felt at ease with each other. You know, Kate, meeting your parents made a perfect ending to a perfect day.'

* * *

Yes, thought Kate as she got ready for bed, it has been a perfect day—well, nearly perfect, she amended. James had asked me to marry him, and I've said yes, and my parents approve. All we want now is our children's approval. Our future is in their hands.

CHAPTER ELEVEN

THERE was no let-up in the hot weather as July merged into August.

The children revelled in it, spending long days on the beach or at the junior tennis club where, as members, they received professional tuition. They went ice-skating and ten pin bowling in Porthampton and met up with friends. They spent occasional days at the White House, being fed and generally spoilt by Mrs Bee, and made forays along the stretch of rugged, wild foreshore that fronted the house to collect all sorts of flotsam and jetsam.

Frequently they visited the nursery and helped to pick and weigh punnets of soft fruit, or bunch cut flowers and water potted plants. They generally made themselves useful there, earning themselves pocket money which gave them immense pleasure.

And, to top everything off, the regular bulletins on Hugo continued to be encouraging, giving a further boost to their happiness.

Altogether, for the four of them, cementing their friendship which had begun on day one, it was an idyllic summer.

But for Kate and James it was, as Mrs Orwell had forecast, a bitter-sweet time. They were pleased that the children were happy, but nail-bitingly frustrated by being in daily contact and having to be discreet. It was agony. The snatched embraces behind their office doors—or the lodge kitchen when the children were in the garden—only emphasised their raw, sexual need for each other.

They both began to look drawn and tired, though this

could have been explained by the fact that they were working incredibly hard.

The continuing influx of summer visitors was putting enormous pressure on the staff of the Memorial, which was depleted—in spite of Kate's efforts to maintain a full rota—by holidays and sickness caused through a rogue virus.

Leaving the inevitable paperwork till the evening, Kate helped out wherever she could, mostly on the medical and long-stay wards which were full, and did any job that needed to be done from bed-making to giving injections.

James worked flat out, too, covering for hard-pressed local doctors. He did much of the elective surgery in the day unit and in Theatre, but he was also much in evidence on the medical wing so that he and Kate were thrown together more than ever.

Feeling the way they did, it was a mixed blessing. Every touch, every look they exchanged, made their blood pressure soar and their pulses race. Kate, seeing the naked desire in his eyes, knew that James was reaching the end of his sexual tether, and she wasn't far behind. She felt a painful, wild longing to be folded in his arms and feel the thrust of him deep inside her.

Her legs, her whole body, ached at the thought, and she knew that soon, very soon, they would have to find time for themselves—no kids, no hospital—just the two of them, as it had been on that fateful Wednesday weeks before.

But their first full day off, toward the end of August, was owed to the children who had, without complaint, entertained themselves for weeks.

Announcing that they were to have a day off, James told them that the choice of where they went was up to them.

'Swathley Castle Adventure Park,' said Tony without hesitation. 'We all want to go there.'

'Yeah, it's brilliant—been advertised on telly—it's got dungeons and things,' enthused Philip.

'And a miniature village, and a lake and boating,' Bess chimed in.'

'*And* there's a fair,' said Sonia.

'With all sorts of fab rides,' added Tony.

'Yeah, like the "beat gravity" ride in the sky,' said Philip.

Their enthusiasm was infectious. 'If we should live that long,' said James dryly as he raised amused eyebrows at Kate, his eyes twinkling.

He looked more relaxed than he had for weeks, and her heart lifted. 'It sounds wonderful,' she said happily. It wasn't perfect as they wouldn't be alone together, but they would be away from the pressures of the hospital for a day and the children would be fun to be with. A family day out—it had a nice ring to it.

Swathley Castle, its round turreted towers dominating the flat landscape of heath and woodland surrounding it, stood—a sturdy fortress—on top of a steep hill.

'Wow, like out of a book,' said Sonia, peering out of the window as James drew up in the car park.

'Romantic—knights in armour,' murmured Bess dreamily.

James, picking up his cue, said with a grin, 'Allow me, my lady.' Bowing over Kate's hand, he helped her out of the car.

She bobbed a curtsy.

Keeping hold of her hand and circling her palm with his thumb, which sent tremors up her arm, he mouthed, 'I love you.' They slowly followed the children out of the car park.

It was a sexy, intimate gesture, and Kate's heart knocked

against her ribs. She whispered. 'Love you, too.'

The children were waiting for them at a signpost, pointing the way to various attractions. 'So where to first?' asked James, looking round at their animated faces.

After a noisy discussion they voted for the fair.

Kate and James chickened out of the Scream a Second Monorail Experience, looping high above the fairground, but took part in the Dangerous Dungeon Challenge and the Virtual Reality Formula 1 racing game.

They left the fair full of candy floss and ice cream, visited the motor museum, took a boat on the lake and watched a jousting match.

It was mid-afternoon when they returned to the car to collect the food hamper and make their way to the picnic area to eat.

The picnic area was a large, grassy clearing, ringed round with trees and dotted about with rustic tables and benches and separated from the car park by a low post and rail fence.

Sitting at a table in the shade of a small oak tree, the children made plans for the rest of the afternoon as they ate their way steadily through the sandwiches, hard-boiled eggs, sausage rolls, fruit tarts and yoghurt that Kate had provided.

James and Kate sat side by side, thighs touching, fleetingly brushing hands and bare arms against each other. They said little, content to exchange tender, loving glances and simply be close to each other as they listened to the noisy, cheerful conversation going on around them.

Cocooned in our love, thought Kate, achingly aware of James's vibratingly warm presence beside her. Hot on its heels came a second sobering thought—or imprisoned by it? No, never that, but I wish like *hell* we could tell the children that we're in love. She looked at their shining, happy, intelligent faces, her heart beating a wild tattoo, and wondered... Was now the time?

She turned her head and met James's eyes, gleaming, penetrating, reading her thoughts. She *looked* her question.

A broad smile slowly lifted the corners of his mouth. He took a deep breath, and said in a low, decisive voice, 'Oh, yes, Kate, *now* is definitely the—'

He stopped abruptly as a piercing shriek rang out from the direction of the car park. As they all turned to pinpoint it the door of a camper van, parked against the low perimeter fence, burst open. A woman with an infant in her arms and a child clinging to her skirt fell out of the doorway, enveloped in smoke.

James was on his feet in an instant and pelting towards the vehicle, which was belching out smoke. A second later Kate followed him, calling over her shoulder to the children to stay put. They had almost reached the huddled figures lying on the ground when there was a fresh roar and crackle and a tongue of flame licked out to join the sombre billowing from the van door.

James made for the woman and baby, who were lying inert, and Kate ran to the small girl, who was screaming.

Bending to pick her up, Kate saw that the hem of her dress was smouldering. Quickly, ignoring the heat, she smothered the fold of burning fabric between her hands.

'It's all right sweetheart,' she soothed, as she lifted the child and began to back away from the fire. The noise and heat were frightening. 'You're not burnt. It's out now.'

A yard away James was hauling the dazed woman to her feet. 'Are you hurt? Is there anyone else inside?' he asked, dragging her away from the vehicle which was now blazing fiercely. She shook her head, tears trickling down her smoke-streaked cheeks. 'No,' she croaked, clutching the baby tightly but sagging helplessly against him as her legs gave way.

James swept her and the infant up in his arms, and rasped, 'Run, Kate. This lot's going to go up any minute.'

Adrenalin lending wings to their feet, they raced back across the clearing. From behind them as they ran came the sharp, ringing report of something exploding, and the air was suddenly full of flying, burning debris and whining pieces of hot metal.

Surprised shouts and cries rang out from the handful of other picnickers as tinder-dry grass and little clumps of bracken began to smoulder. In a second a dozen small fires had sprung up all about them and thick, acrid smoke, fanned by the breeze, swirled round their heads.

They were coughing and their eyes were streaming by the time they reached the far edge of the picnic area where the children were waiting. The smoke hadn't got that far. The wind was blowing away from them. The children were tense but composed.

'What shall we do, Dad?' asked Tony.

James said with quiet urgency,' Decide which direction to take and then move as fast as possible.' He lowered the woman onto the bench as he spoke, and she struggled to her feet. 'Thank you. I can walk now,' she choked out, but swayed uncertainly. She looked very pale, if she might faint at any minute.

James kept his arm round her waist and said briskly, 'Kate, you take her other side. Tony, you and Philip piggy-back the little girl. Bess, Sonia, you take turns carrying the baby. Don't wait for us. Go ahead, and follow this path up to the left away from the wind. It's smoke we have to worry about most. With luck there'll be some help coming soon. There's a first-aid station near the entrance — make for that.'

Kate thought that the woman might refuse to hand over the baby, but she didn't. She just said tiredly, 'Thank you, you're very kind.'

The children didn't argue either but did as James had instructed, marching off smartly as soon as the baby had been handed over, though Bess gave Kate an anguished look as she set off with the whimpering infant in her arms. In a few minutes they had outstripped Kate and James and had disappeared round a bend in the path.

Let them be safe, Kate prayed and, meeting James's eyes, knew that he was doing the same.

The path, which had started off as a gentle slope, grew steeper and time became irrelevant to Kate as she and James struggled up the crumbling, dusty dirt path with the badly shocked, exhausted woman between them, dragging one foot after another. Minutes seemed like hours.

There were several more loud explosions, and the whistling sound of debris flying through the air. Glancing back through the trees, they saw that the fire was now raging over much of the picnic area. A pall of shifting smoke hung over it. An overwhelming stench of burning metal, vegetation and timber drifted up the hillside.

Something heavy landed in the undergrowth a few yards away from them. A faint wisp of smoke spiralled upwards, and the dry leaves of a dying fern crackled as small, darting flames licked round it. So the fire had begun to reach this far! Where would it end? Would the woods go up in flames? Were the children safe? Kate and James exchanged shocked glances.

James said grimly, 'Wait there.' Leaving her to support the woman, he streaked toward the spot and stamped viciously on the smouldering plant. He was back within seconds.

'You go ahead, Kate,' he said. 'We'll manage.'

'No!'

He wasn't sending her on to safety as he had the children. Her place was with him. And, strong as he was, he would have difficulty in practically carrying this tall, big-boned female up the steep path with its crumbling surface. He needed her help, minimal as it might be.

He dredged up a glimmer of a smile, and said dryly, 'Stubborn as ever, Kate. Come on, then, let's push on.'

As he spoke there came the wail of fire sirens from below in the valley and the sound of voices from the path above. It was a wonderful sound. Help was at hand, and within minutes they were able to hand over the care of their patient to two burly St John's Ambulance men, who urged them to get themselves down to the first-aid station.

'You've done enough,' one of them said. 'Look as if you could do with a breather.'

'That's for sure,' said James. 'Come on, love, let's go find the kids.' He grasped Kate's hand firmly. She winced. 'What's wrong?' he asked sharply.

'Nothing much. My hands are a bit sore.'

James turned them over. 'They're burnt,' he said angrily. 'And you've been hauling that woman around.'

'It wasn't too bad—my arms did much of the work. It's just that you squeezed my hand so tightly.'

'The sooner you get dressings on those the better,' he said, and, kissing her swiftly, pushed her up the slope before him.

It was late afternoon when they were eventually allowed to return to the car park to retrieve their car.

They were on a high—curiously elated, happy, conscious of the fact that they had survived a shared danger. A danger which had been short-lived but which might have resulted in tragedy. Just for a while they had all been at risk. Love flowed all round them, embraced them. It made the children noisy and boisterous and Kate and James quiet and thoughtful.

It had been a miracle that no one had been badly hurt, and only the little family they had rescued had been sent to hospital for a check-up—suffering from shock and mild smoke inhalation, the first-aid staff told them. Otherwise, there had been a few minor burns, like Kate's blistered hands, that had needed treatment.

And it had been a further miracle what the woods hadn't caught fire, thought Kate as they stood by the car, gazing across the park. If they had... She shuddered.

James, seeming to share the thought, took her bandaged hand gently and raised it to his lips. 'We're incredibly lucky,' he said softly. 'Everyone's safe and sound. It might have been so much worse.'

'Yes,' she agreed. 'Much worse.'

The car park was half-empty. The far corner, where the fire had occurred had been cordoned off and nearby cars removed. A fire engine was still standing guard over the burnt-out shells of the camper van and the cars on either side of it. The picnic area beyond was a flat black mass of steaming stubble. Many of the tables and benches were charred or completely burnt, but *their* bench beneath the oak tree appeared untouched.

Even the children stared at it for a moment in awed silence.

'It's like an omen,' said Sonia solemnly.

Tony and Philip said, 'Yeah, sort of.' They punched each other's shoulders in the embarrassed fashion that only young lads exhibit.

Kate thought, It's lovely to see them behaving like kids—I don't want them to grow up too soon.

Bess pointed up at the grey, castellated towers of

Swathley Castle, just visible over the treetops. 'We never did get up to see the castle,' she said with a sigh. 'And it's so romantic.'

'There's no reason why we shouldn't come back next year,' said James as they all piled into the car. 'But right now let's move. We've had enough adventures for one day.'

A policeman stopped them at the exit gates. 'Just checking that everyone's accounted for, sir,' he said, as James pulled up. 'May I have your name and address—just a formality in case we need to contact you for further information?'

'Dr James Bruce, The White House, Sea Lane, Lower Millchester, Sussex.'

'And this is your family?' asked the officer, nodding at Kate and the children.

'Well, not exactly,' Kate explained with a quirky smile. 'Half of them are mine. . .' She trailed off, catching the expression in James's eyes.

'As of this moment,' he said, and his voice was deadly serious, 'but I hope soon to remedy that. There is, you might say, a merger in the offing.'

Kate gave a choking, startled gasp, and said breathily, 'James!'

He slid her a loving, sideways glance. 'It's the right time, Kate,' he said.

Slowly, with her heart hammering, Kate turned to look at the children.

They were sitting motionless, dead silent, their astonished eyes fixed on the back of James's head.

They hate the idea, Kate thought. It's too soon. We should have broken it to them more gently. Her stomach went cold. What have we done?

Then quite suddenly the children were all talking at once.

'Great!'

'Brilliant!'

'Utterly fantastic.'

'Cool!'

Bess leant forward, hugged her and said, 'It's the best thing that could have happened. I do love you, Mum.' Straining at their seat belt, she kissed James on the cheek, and added, 'And I love you, too. You're positively the nicest man I know. I'm glad you're going to be our stepfather and we're all going to be one big family.'

James said gruffly, his eyes suspiciously bright, 'Thank you, Bess. That's the nicest thing you could say to me. I'll try to live up to it.'

Kate's felt that she would burst with joy. She loved them all so much, the children and this strong and gentle man, sitting beside her. She stretched out her bandaged hand and stroked his cheek where Bess had kissed it, and said with teasing tenderness, 'Oh, you'll live up to it, my darling. You'll be the best husband and father in the world.' She looked over her shoulder. 'Won't he, kids?'

'Utterly the best,' said the girls with beaming smiles.

'Wicked,' said Tony.

'Real cool,' said Philip laconically.

And that, thought Kate, is praise indeed, and sighed with absolute contentment.

4 FREE
books and a surprise gift!

We would like to take this opportunity to thank you for reading this Mills & Boon® book by offering you the chance to take FOUR more specially selected titles from the Medical Romance™ series absolutely FREE! We're also making this offer to introduce you to the benefits of the Reader Service™—

- ★ FREE home delivery
- ★ FREE gifts and competitions
- ★ FREE monthly newsletter
- ★ Books available before they're in the shops
- ★ Exclusive Reader Service discounts

Accepting these FREE books and gift places you under no obligation to buy, you may cancel at any time, even after receiving your free shipment. Simply complete your details below and return the entire page to the address below. *You don't even need a stamp!*

YES! Please send me 4 free Medical Romance books and a surprise gift. I understand that unless you hear from me, I will receive 4 superb new titles every month for just £2.30 each, postage and packing free. I am under no obligation to purchase any books and may cancel my subscription at any time. The free books and gift will be mine to keep in any case.

M8XE

Ms/Mrs/Miss/Mr..................................Initials ....
BLOCK CAPITALS PLEASE

Surname ....

Address ....

....

....Postcode................................

Send this whole page to:
THE READER SERVICE, FREEPOST, CROYDON, CR9 3WZ
(Eire readers please send coupon to: P.O. BOX 4546, DUBLIN 24.)

Offer not valid to current Reader Service subscribers to this series. We reserve the right to refuse an application and applicants must be aged 18 years or over. Only one application per household. Terms and prices subject to change without notice. Offer expires 30th September 1998. You may be mailed with offers from other reputable companies as a result of this application. If you would prefer not to receive such offers, please tick box. ☐
Mills & Boon® Medical Romance™ is a registered trademark of Harlequin Mills & Boon Ltd.

MILLS & BOON

Medical Romance

COMING NEXT MONTH

SOMEONE ELSE'S BABY by Jean Evans

All Neil was asking of her was friendship but Beth knew that accepting would be a lie. After all her feelings had little to do with friendship.

DANIEL'S DILEMMA by Maggie Kingsley

Daniel had already tried marriage once and he thought it would take a miracle to get him to try it again. And then he met Rebecca...

FROM THIS DAY FORWARD
by Laura MacDonald

Book 2 in the Matchmaker Quartet

Kate had a successful professional life but she fell apart when it came to men! She doubted that Jon would be the one to alter that, but he had other ideas.

A LITTLE BIT OF MAGIC by Josie Metcalfe

When Penny turns up, Dare thinks that she is following him. Little does he realise that she is his new nurse. After such a bad start Penny was determined that things could only get better.

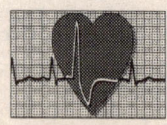

On Sale from   **6th April 1998**

Available at most branches of WH Smith, John Menzies, Martins, Tesco, Volume One and Safeway

MILLS & BOON®

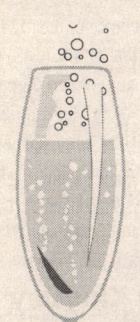

THREE BRIDES, NO GROOM

BY
DEBBIE MACOMBER

We are delighted to bring you three brand-new stories about love and marriage from one of our most popular authors.

Even though the caterers were booked, the bouquets bought and the bridal dresses were ready to wear...the grooms suddenly got cold feet. And that's when three women decided they weren't going to get mad...they were going to get even!

On sale from 6th April 1998
Price £5.25

Available at most branches of WH Smith, John Menzies, Martins, Tesco, Asda, Volume One, Sainsbury and Safeway

MILLS & BOON

SILHOUETTE®

SPECIAL OFFER £5 OFF

FLYING FLOWERS

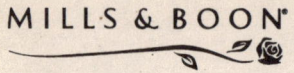

Beautiful fresh flowers, sent by 1st class post to any UK and Eire address.

We have teamed up with Flying Flowers, the UK's premier 'flowers by post' company, to offer you £5 off a choice of their two most popular bouquets the 18 mix (CAS) of 10 multihead and 8 luxury bloom Carnations and the 25 mix (CFG) of 15 luxury bloom Carnations, 10 Freesias and Gypsophila. All bouquets contain fresh flowers 'in bud', added greenery, bouquet wrap, flower food, care instructions, and personal message card. They are boxed, gift wrapped and sent by 1st class post.

To redeem £5 off a Flying Flowers bouquet, simply complete the application form below and send it with your cheque or postal order to; **HMB Flying Flowers Offer, The Jersey Flower Centre, Jersey JE1 5FF.**

ORDER FORM (Block capitals please) Valid for delivery anytime until 30th November 1998 MAB/0298/A

Title .... Initials .... Surname ....

Address ....

....

.... Postcode ....

Signature .... Are you a Reader Service Subscriber **YES/NO**

Bouquet(s) **18 CAS** (Usual Price £14.99) **£9.99** ☐   **25 CFG** (Usual Price £19.99) **£14.99** ☐

I enclose a cheque/postal order payable to Flying Flowers for £ .... or payment by

VISA/MASTERCARD ☐☐☐☐ ☐☐☐☐ ☐☐☐☐ ☐☐☐☐ Expiry Date ..../........./........

PLEASE SEND MY BOUQUET TO ARRIVE BY ..../........./........

TO Title .... Initials .... Surname ....

Address ....

....

.... Postcode ....

Message (Max 10 Words) ....

....

Please allow a minimum of four working days between receipt of order and 'required by date' for delivery.

You may be mailed with offers from other reputable companies as a result of this application. Please tick box if you would prefer not to receive such offers. ☐

Terms and Conditions Although dispatched by 1st class post to arrive by the required date the exact day of delivery cannot be guaranteed. Valid for delivery anytime until 30th November 1998. Maximum of 5 redemptions per household, photocopies of the voucher will be accepted.